Henry Francis Colby

A Tribute to the Memory of Ebenezer Thresher

Henry Francis Colby

A Tribute to the Memory of Ebenezer Thresher

ISBN/EAN: 9783741193415

Manufactured in Europe, USA, Canada, Australia, Japa

Cover: Foto ©Andreas Hilbeck / pixelio.de

Manufactured and distributed by brebook publishing software
(www.brebook.com)

Henry Francis Colby

A Tribute to the Memory of Ebenezer Thresher

TO THE MEMORY OF

Ebenezer Thresher.

BY

HENRY F. COLBY, D. D.,

PASTOR OF THE FIRST BAPTIST CHURCH, DAYTON, OHIO.

DAYTON, OHIO:
Press of United Brethren Publishing House.
1886.

EBENEZER THRESHER.

BENEZER THRESHER was born in Stafford, Connecticut, on the thirty-first day of August, 1798. His ancestors on his father's side, he thought, were of German descent. His grandparents were Christopher Thresher, who died in 1779, and Thankful Thomas. These had eight children, of whom the third, Ebenezer, married Hannah, the daughter of Joshua Blodgett. The Blodgetts are said to have descended from French Huguenots. Hannah Blodgett's mother was an Alden, and her lineage is traceable to John Alden of the Mayflower. The subject of this memoir was the ninth of the twelve children of Ebenezer and Hannah Blodgett Thresher. Of these children two died in childhood. The remainder grew up and lived to a good old age.

A few years before his death, at the earnest request of the writer, and for the gratification of his family, Mr. Thresher wrote down some memoranda of his early life. Concerning this period, therefore, it will be interesting to let the narrative proceed substantially in his own language. Only those verbal changes have been made which seemed desirable to adapt the paper to its present use, and which, it is believed, he would himself have approved.

He says: "My family were among the virtuous poor. My father was bred to the business of farming, and owned a farm. He possessed a good constitution and had a well-developed physical frame. He was also a man of great strength. By excessive labor, however, in the heat of summer he broke down, and was afterward afflicted with asthma in its most distressing form, which disqualified him for active labor. His feeble health, with a young and numerous family, compelled him to borrow money for their support, so that his estate in a few years became loaded with mortgages for all it was worth. The condition of the family rendered it necessary for my two elder brothers, as soon as they were able to earn something, to go from home, for the purpose of redeeming the farm, the scanty product of which was the family's only means of support. Meanwhile I was left with the care of the farm and of the family at the age of twelve years, with such assistance as my sisters, older than myself, could give me. My mother was a woman of delicate health. She was a member of a Baptist church. She first united with the Baptist Church in the adjoining town of Willington, at a distance from her home of eight or ten miles, but when the Baptist Church in Stafford was organized, in

1809), she became a constituent member of it. My father never united with any church, but was, I believe, for many years before his death, a Christian man. He was a man of great courage, but of tender feelings and refined sensibilities. He was just and honorable in all his dealings, and particularly regardful of the rights of others. My parents were intelligent for their opportunities and gave their children all the advantages that their means would allow. We had a village school three months in summer for small children, taught by a school-mistress, and one three months in the winter taught by a master. In these schools no branches were taught but reading, writing, spelling, and arithmetic as far as the Rule of Three. I attended school for the most part three months in each year, but such were my engrossments until I was eighteen years of age, and so excessive were my cares and labors for one of my age, that I had little time for thought or study except in these school-hours. Sunday-schools had not yet been established in that part of the country. As we lived four and six miles distant from any regular places of worship, my attendance at Sabbath-services was extremely irregular. Even if I had had more leisure, there was nothing in my circumstances to lead me to literary pursuits, even to reading. I do not recollect to have seen, until I was eighteen years of age, any other books besides my school-books, the Bible, Pilgrim's Progress, and Watts' Psalms and Hymns. The population was sparse, and all the people, being relatively poor, were, like myself, engrossed in providing for themselves the necessary means of living.

"It had been arranged that I should be released from the care of the family at the age of eighteen, and that I should then be entitled to my own earnings, an elder brother then taking my place in the household. The winter of 1817 was to be my last at the neighboring school and in the shelter of my paternal home. In the following spring I was expecting to embark on the sea of life, sailing by my own compass. It seemed to me to be a vast ocean, and in what port I might land was to me a matter of the utmost uncertainty. And yet I was hopeful. I felt a persuasion that there was some place for me in the world. But it was during that winter or early in the following spring that I experienced a great change in my religious views and feelings. Up to that period I do not recollect to have had any decided convictions of my sinfulness in the sight of God. During this entire winter I had more or less of this feeling, which culminated in very great distress of mind. It led me to seek refuge in the Lord Jesus Christ. I know of no instrumentality employed in producing this change but the Spirit of God. The realization to which I have alluded, that I had reached a critical point in my life, had made me thoughtful and somewhat solicitous, and God was pleased in his infinite goodness to send to me his Spirit to be my guide. He had prepared a shower of divine grace for that region of country, which was poured out in great abundance. It seems to have been bestowed in answer to the united prayers of three individuals. It transpired that two female members of the Baptist Church and one male member of a Methodist Church held by agreement a prayer-meeting to pray for a revival of religion. My own mother was one of the number and her brother was another. This prayer-meeting was unknown to me, and, as far as I was ever informed, to all but themselves. They were led to hold it by their reflections on the low state of religious feeling in the community. Another young man in the neighborhood had been converted before I was; but this fact also was unknown to me at the time.

"A desire was soon expressed for meetings to be held at private houses. These became frequent, then were held every night and were attended by large numbers. More would assemble than could find seats or standing room in the house, many gathering around the door-way and windows. Conversions became frequent, and the meetings were carried on chiefly by those recently converted. Great quietness and solemnity prevailed. The small Baptist church at Stafford was at this time without a pastor and had no public house of worship. They held occasional meetings in private houses in a distant part of the town where most of the members resided. This revival soon extended into contiguous neighborhoods and into adjoining towns, but was confined mostly to rural districts remote from the centers of population and among people who had seldom attended religious worship. My time during these months was given up to attendance on these meetings, in which I generally participated with others in reading the Scriptures, singing, prayer, and exhortation.

"The change which I had experienced in my religious views and this engrossment in meetings, in which the object particularly sought was the conversion of others, altered entirely the plan of my life. Hitherto I had been considering only how I could advance my own personal interests. Now my study was how to do the most good to others. I had evidence that I had a treasure in heaven upon the possession of which I should soon enter. Time seemed short and precious. I had food and raiment (although I was poorly clad) and was therewith content, for it seemed to me altogether uncertain whether I should need anything more. I was received into the fellowship of the small church in Stafford by baptism in March, 1817.

"The time set for my leaving home had already passed, but I felt a reluctance to leave scenes which had been so intensely interesting to me. About the first of April I hired myself out to a neighboring farmer for the coming season at twelve dollars a month. Richard

Gardner, my employer, and his amiable wife were pious people. They were very considerate of me and extremely kind. This season of easy cares and moderate labor was for me a period of intense study how I could best subserve the interests of the kingdom of Christ. I became very sensible of my need of more learning than I then possessed, the attainment of which I determined should be my first object of pursuit. This to me in my ignorance and indigence was a pretty heavy undertaking. I knew almost nothing of institutions of learning or of the methods of education. I resolved to lay aside my earnings for a few years and then expend them in obtaining instruction. Having obtained through a friend employment in the city of New Haven at better wages than I could obtain nearer home, I left for that city in the early spring of 1818, with my extemporized knapsack containing my wardrobe of homespun. I made the journey of sixty miles on foot in two days. My employer had a small farm adjacent to the city, of which I was to have the care. After fulfilling this engagement, which was one of excessive labor, I obtained employment with a wealthy gentleman in the city at better wages and for easier service. I had the care of his garden and of his carriage and horses which I drove when occasion required. In this family I was treated with kindness; the lady especially, who was a Christian woman, was very considerate toward me. No service was re-

quired of me in the evenings. This enabled me to add
to my pecuniary resources by sawing wood on moon-
light evenings.

"When I came to New Haven I found a small Baptist church. With this I at once identified myself.
It consisted of about thirty members, mostly women,
and all relatively poor. They had no pastor, but assembled regularly for worship in a small hired room
owned by a Congregational church. This was then the
only Baptist church in the city. We succeeded in organizing a Sunday-school, and during the two years
I lived there I think the church had some substantial
growth. When I left I succeeded in sending them a
pastor, Rev. Benjamin M. Hill, whose ministry was
greatly blessed in building up the Baptist cause in
New Haven. He came from the church in Stafford,
where he had been ordained as pastor, a year or two
before. After leaving New Haven he was pastor at
Troy, New York, and then for twenty-two years was
secretary of the American Baptist Home Mission Society.

"By this time my knowledge of the world had become somewhat enlarged, and I had learned something
by reading. The Bible, however, was my chief book of
study. I had never had the opportunity of mingling
with people of literary tastes and acquirements; and
in those days facilities for acquiring knowledge were
limited. The days of my childhood and youth were

passed before there was a religious newspaper published
in the country. The Baptist people with whom I associated did not appreciate the advantages of a liberal
education for the ministry. The Baptist minister with
whom I was most intimate stoutly opposed my plan
of seeking an education, and told me, as his last ar-
gument, that he once knew a young man who entered
upon a course of college education for the ministry
but died before he had completed it. This considera-
bly affected me. It even influenced my dreams. I
once dreamed of passing through the article of death.
By prayerful thought, however, I rose above this difficulty.

"I did not at first anticipate a collegiate education.
My age—I had now entered my twenty-second year—
and my lack of early advantages seemed to preclude
it. I concluded to seek the guidance of a private
teacher, and preferred a minister of the gospel. I had
heard of Rev. Jonathan Going, the pastor of the Baptist church in Worcester, Massachusetts, as a man of
liberal education and interested in young men. I determined to apply to him for instruction. Having returned to my native place, I traveled on foot from
Stafford, Connecticut, to Worcester, Massachusetts, a distance of about thirty miles, on the nineteenth day of
April, 1820."

From these personal reminiscences it will be seen
that a burden of care and anxiety rested upon Mr.

Thresher's youth. But these seemed only to develop
the independence and energy of his character. He illus-
trated the saying that for noble and ambitious natures
hardships in youth are like the walls of a cannon
giving direction and effectiveness to the force which
they inclose and restrain. Among the influences which
shaped his character we discern also that mother's
earnest piety, which led her to join with her brother
and neighbor in petitions for an outpouring of the
Holy Spirit, petitions that were rewarded by the religious revival of the whole community and especially
by the conversion of her own boy. How many forces
for good in this world are traceable to maternal counsels and prayers! And how does that little and humble
prayer-meeting illustrate the small and often unseen
beginnings from which in God's providence large issues
spring! Moreover, we are reminded here how awakening and enlarging to the mind is often the effect of a
thorough conversion of the heart to Christ! A new and
exalted motive is thus realized which, if humbly followed, develops the man's best powers, and guides him
into paths of broader usefulness. As from the church
in Stafford, feeble enough in that day, came Ebenezer
Thresher, so from many other country churches, where
hard-working but intelligent people have feared God
and studied their Bibles, have come men whose power
has been felt as conscientious and earnest workers in
the church or in the state. This not only commends

religion and gives great encouragement to boys of apparently few advantages, but it is an incentive to religious effort in rural communities. These may be inconspicuous but sure sources to supply leaders for many a noble cause. While our cities clamor for evangelization, it is the part of Christian wisdom to sow broadcast gospel truth and strong convictions in country places also. How little our subject knew · what was before him when he started out from his home!

A Christian engraver has said that the great impression of his life was made by a print of a boy with a bundle on his back leaving home, while God's Spirit asks, "Whither?" Happy the youth who, like the subject of these pages, going forth to untried scenes, invokes that Spirit to be his guide! It is remarkable that he should have formed so clear and strong a desire for an education when there was absolutely nothing, as far as we can see, in his environment to awaken or encourage it. His choice of a church in New Haven, where other denominations had so much strength, evinced the independence and firmness of his doctrinal convictions, while his consecration to his divine Master was manifested and developed by the humble work he tried to do in his name.

He subsequently visited his early home only at long intervals. The following extract taken from a letter written to his brother James in 1829 has now a pathetic interest: "On a certain morning I was filled

with a peculiar sensation at the sight of father as I
viewed him at a distance, from the eminence north of
the house, which you will readily call to mind. I saw
him an old man leaning upon his staff. I reflected
upon his hardships and his sickness, and from this I
reflected upon the toils, the hardships, and disappoint-
ments of life generally; that in a few days I should
be an old man like my father, or sleeping in my
grave." His father, here spoken of as so infirm, died
in 1832, at the age of seventy-six. His mother did
not die till eight years later, when she was about
eighty. To his older brothers Mr. Thresher was indebted for kindness and material aid while he was
struggling to obtain his education. As these left home
before he did, and before the youngest of the family
circle were old enough to come to the family table, a
remarkable occurrence was rendered possible. In 1875,
when Mr. Thresher visited Stafford for the last time,
he met and sat down to eat with three sisters and
two brothers. They had never all sat down to the table together before in their lives, and yet the average
age of the six was more than eighty years. Three of
that company are still living. May the smile of Heaven
rest on their closing years!

The day after his arrival at Worcester, Mr. Thresher
commenced the study of geography and English gram-
mar. He says, continuing his narrative: "Dr. Going
received me very cordially, and took me into his

family and promised to give me such instructions as
his other engagements would allow. I resided with
him some three or four months. It was a season of
deepest interest to me, an epoch in the history of my
life, in which I made great discoveries. There was
another young man in Dr. Going's family named
Whitman Metcalf, who, like myself, had sought his instructions. As far as recitations were concerned we became mutual instructors, for Dr. Going did not much
relish the drudgery of recitations. When I arrived in
Worcester it was in the afternoon, the sun being yet
far up in the heavens. Before the sun went down
Metcalf invited me to go with him into a distant field
for prayer. The invitation was cheerfully accepted.
Metcalf was then a married man and was able to obtain only a limited education, but he became an eminently useful Baptist minister. Dr. Going was a good
adviser but a poor teacher. He was not a man of
details but of bold conceptions, genial in temperament
and of boundless benevolence. His conversations and
advice were of great service to me. I was now brought
also into an intelligent Baptist community. I attended
the Baptist ministers' meetings in Worcester County,
which were very useful to me. While in Worcester I
supported myself by laboring occasionally for neighboring farmers, which enabled me to retain my muscular
strength. Deacon Stowell remarked to his pastor that
that student could handle a scythe better than any

man he had before known. While in Worcester my mind became enlarged. I was made still more sensible of my deficiencies, and I determined to seek a collegiate education. I have never ceased to adore the goodness of divine Providence in leading me to Jonathan Going, whose intimacy I enjoyed while he lived, and who in the later years of his life sought my advice as often as I did his."

It is worthy of note at this point that eleven years afterward this same Dr. Going, to whom Mr. Thresher here refers so affectionately, after an influential pastorate at Worcester, during which Sunday-schools, foreign missions, and ministerial education found in him an earnest advocate, visited Ohio, attended the meeting of the Western Baptist Convention at Lancaster, on May 25, 1831, and rendered useful aid in maturing the plans for the establishment of a literary and theological institution at Granville. In the conventions of 1833 and 1834 it was preëminently his counsel and influence which shaped and carried the plan for the Western Baptist Education Society which was then formed. In 1837, after serving for five years as secretary of the Home Mission Society, he became the second president of Granville, and greatly increased the prosperity of that school of Christian learning. His death, in 1844, was regarded as a great loss to Ohio Baptists. Possibly his connection with Granville may have been among the influences which deepened the

17

interest in that college, since known as Denison University, which Mr. Thresher afterward manifested, having come to Ohio in the year following Dr. Going's death. When, visiting Granville in recent years as an aged man, he may have looked upon the monument which marks in the college cemetery the grave of his early counselor and friend, how must it have brought up to his mind those old days at Worcester, Massachusetts, when, a humble aspirant for Christian learning, he first knocked at the good man's door! Little, too, at that early day, did Dr. Going think that he was helping to start on his course a friend of education who in future days would not only greatly promote that cause at the east, but would come after himself and strengthen by his gifts and influence the foundations of an institution which the former should help establish in this western and then far distant state! Nor let us fail to note that the fellow-student Mr. Thresher speaks of as bowing with himself in prayer, Whitman Metcalf, afterward manifested a similar zeal for the cause of missions and of Christian learning. He was recognized as a religious leader in western New York, and became widely known through a long life as a missionary, a pastor, a builder of churches, the secretary of the New York Baptist Convention, and the financial agent of the New York Baptist Education Society. How many streams of enlightening influences have flowed from the conversa-

2

tions in his study and at his table of that New England pastor with those two poor but earnest young men! Sir Humphrey Davy said that his greatest discovery was his pupil, Michael Faraday. Not the least among the elements of Dr. Going's usefulness must be reckoned the direction he gave to the lives of Whitman Metcalf and Ebenezer Thresher.

It was soon evident, however, that, with all its advantages, Dr. Going's home was not the place to pursue classical learning. He therefore sought the instruction of Rev. Abiel Fisher, pastor of the Baptist church in Bellingham, Massachusetts, who had under his instruction several young men whom he was fitting for college. With Mr. Fisher he commenced the study of Latin. After a few months he determined on another change. "I became satisfied," he said, "that my advantages in a quiet country town, under a private tutor who could give but a limited amount of time to his scholars, were not equal to what I could find in a good academy. I consequently removed from Bellingham to Amherst, and entered Amherst Academy in the spring of 1821, where I remained in close attention to my studies until the fall of 1823." This academy had been incorporated five years previous. Noah Webster, LL. D., was one of its trustees. He was residing at Amherst, engaged in the preparation of his great dictionary at the time our subject came to the place as a student. Dr. Webster was also active as one of the founders and the first president of the board of trustees of Amherst College, which was started that same year. In another reference to this period of his own life Mr. Thresher says: "I early began to cherish the hope that I might at some time be permitted to preach the Gospel. Having in my early Christian experience, by a kind of necessity, been called into active duty in meetings for worship, I continued these habits as opportunities offered during my course of education. In Amherst there was at that time no Baptist church, but prayer-meetings were maintained by students in the academy. Only two young men besides myself were Baptists, John Pratt and Ephraim Simonds. Pratt and myself were from Connecticut, and Simonds from Massachusetts, the son of a Baptist minister. We all three spent our vacations while at Amherst in assisting feeble churches in adjoining towns."

The John Pratt he here refers to continued to be his classmate until their graduation from college, and was the same who afterward became the first president of the Granville Literary and Theological Institution in Ohio (now Denison University), and whose happy face and patriarchal beard will be readily recalled by many readers of these pages. He resigned the presidency in 1837, to be succeeded by Dr. Going, but continued to work as a vigorous and honored teacher in the college till 1859, when he retired to private life and lived till 1882. Here again we see

another of those early associations which had drawn
Mr. Thresher's attention, even before he came to Ohio,
to the institution of learning to which he became such
a friend. Among his other fellow-students in Amherst
academy at the time referred to, who are worthy of
note for the record of their after-lives, may be mentioned Prof. E. S. Snell, for fifty-three years one of the
chief pillars of Amherst College, Dr. Joseph S. Clark,
for eighteen years secretary of the Massachusetts Home
Missionary Society, Rev. Stephen Johnson, for twenty
years missionary to Siam and China, and Rev. Reu-
ben Tinker, missionary to the Sandwich Islands.

"In the month of January, 1824," the narrative continues, "I entered the freshman class in Columbian
College, Washington. Two considerations influenced me
more particularly in selecting this as the place of my
future studies. One was the prospect of procuring there
some pecuniary assistance. The other was an opportunity of obtaining a better knowledge of the world and
of the forms and usages of society, in which I knew myself to be sadly deficient. My opportunities for study
at Amherst were excellent. The academy was then in
a flourishing condition. Its number of students was
large, and a considerable portion of them were study-
ing for the ministry. I was brought into associations
with persons of literary tastes. Most of the students
belonged to other denominations, which in many respects was an advantage to me. Amherst was at that

time attracting the attention of literary people as a seat of learning, and had been selected as the site of a college. But I had never been far from home and had never been much in cultivated society. Although I knew very well that I should be subjected to many mortifications, I knew equally well it was the thing I needed."

Another fact which probably had an influence in directing Mr. Thresher's steps to Columbian College was its connection with the foreign missionary movement, which for some years had been awakening great interest in the Baptist denomination, and especially with the name of Luther Rice. It was in 1812, when the subject of this memoir was fourteen years of age, that this celebrated man and Rev. Adoniram Judson and wife had become Baptists while on their way to India, sent out by the American Board of Commissioners for Foreign Missions. After they had been baptized by English Baptists in Calcutta, it was agreed that Mr. Rice, being unmarried, should return to this country and urge upon the Baptist denomination the adoption of the work of foreign missions which Providence had thus so remarkably placed in their hands, while Mr. and Mrs. Judson should proceed to locate a mission-station among the heathen. Mr. Rice arrived in this country early in the autumn of 1813.

Mr. Thresher says: "A few of our churches had been brought into sympathy and co-operation before this with our English brethren, who had commenced a mission in India in 1793. Two societies had been formed, one in Salem and one in Boston in 1812, for 'propagating the Gospel in India and other foreign parts.' These two societies appointed Mr. Rice, on his return to this country, as their agent to proceed to New York and Philadelphia for the purpose of awakening the Baptists to united action for the support of a foreign mission. His work resulted in the formation at Philadelphia, on the 18th of May, 1814, of the General Convention of the Baptist Denomination in the United States for Foreign Missions, afterward known as the Triennial Convention. These were startling events. Luther Rice was regarded almost as an angel flying through the midst of heaven calling upon Baptists to be aware of their opportunity and responsibility. The number of Baptist communicants in the United States did not then exceed two hundred thousand. Mr. Rice had almost unbounded influence over the denomination in its comparative feebleness. But he had more enterprise than wisdom, and undertook more than one man could accomplish. He attempted not only to provide means for carrying on foreign missions, but also to superintend the educational interests of the denomination. When he came home from India, the only literary institution of considerable importance in the denomination was Brown University, and it was still poor. We had in the ministry very few men possessing the literary attainments needful in a missionary to the heathen. We had no periodical literature to speak of, except the *Massachusetts Missionary Magazine*, which had been commenced in 1803. The *Christian Watchman*, the first Baptist weekly paper, was not begun till 1818. The entire country was poor, having had a national existence of less than half a century, during which period it had passed through two wars."

Mr. Rice was struck with the deep hold which the views he had been led to receive had taken on the popular mind, but he found no institution whose special mission was to train young men to defend those views at home and abroad. A knowledge of Greek and Hebrew seemed indispensable to those who would translate the Scriptures on the foreign field. The conviction thus took possession of his mind that the Baptists ought to have at least one central theological seminary, and Washington City seemed to him to be the place. The Baptist General Convention took the new enterprise under its supervision, and appointed Mr. Rice financial agent and treasurer; and thus Columbian College was established. It was opened for students in 1822. Indeed the missionary movement not only drew the churches into closer unity and promoted their devotion, but it seems to have been a great stimulus to the founding of institutions of learning. Within about ten years from the time of the formation of the Baptist General Convention and the rise of missionary zeal, no

less than five Baptist institutions of learning, which
have grown into colleges and theological seminaries,
were founded: at Hamilton, New York, 1819; Waterville, Maine, 1820; Washington, District of Columbia,
1822; Georgetown, Kentucky, 1824; Newton, Massachusetts, 1825. When the last named was founded the
theological department in Columbian College was no
longer thought necessary. It must be noted how the
development of one part of the work of Christ's serv-
ants in the world always quickens every other part,
and especially how obedience to his Great Commission
quickens the whole.

The events referred to made a deep impression upon Mr. Thresher's thoughtful mind, as the news was
from time to time discussed among the Baptists of his
acquaintance. "Mr. Rice," he says, "rendered eminent
service to the denomination and deserves to be held
in grateful remembrance by us. He was the means of
calling out a great many young men into the pursuit
of learning and the service of Christ. A large company by his instrumentality were brought into Columbian College from the north and from the south." It
will be observed that the college was opened only a
year or two before Mr. Thresher completed his preparatory studies at Amherst.

In a letter written to his brother just after his arrival at Washington, he congratulates himself on the
speed of his journey. It had taken him three days

from New Haven. "Probably," he says, "there are not elsewhere as good facilities for traveling the same distance as between Washington and Boston. With the exception of a few miles of land carriage, there is steamboat communication from Baltimore to New York City; thence to New Haven." He was pleased with his reception and with the men with whom he was brought in contact. The eloquent Dr. William Staughton, who had been so long a pastor in Philadelphia, was president of the college. Irah Chase, Alva Woods, William Ruggles, and Alexis Caswell were professors while he was there. James D. Knowles and Thomas J. Conant gave instruction as tutors. Among his fellow-students, who have since been well-known and honored in the denomination, were Robert W. Cushman, Baron Stow, R. B. Howell, Joseph T. Robert, Robert Ryland, and John Pratt. The last named was his room-mate. When he entered college James Monroe was president of the United States. He must have witnessed the enthusiastic reception given to LaFayette in Washington in 1824. Before he left Washington, John Quincy Adams had succeeded to the presidency. "I more than realized," he writes, "the social advantages which I had anticipated by my residence in Washington. The opportunity given to the students occasionally for visiting Congress and the sessions of the Supreme Court was of great advantage to me I enjoyed especially my visits to the latter. John Marshall, of Virginia, was then Chief Justice. The dignity of the judges, the courteous manners of the advocates, and the supremacy of law greatly impressed me. In my first year in college Henry Clay was speaker of the House of Representatives; and I heard Daniel Webster, then a new member, make his maiden speech in favor of rendering assistance to the Greeks. Both houses of Congress at that period contained a large number of men of distinguished ability.

"The first year I was in college the Christian students brought the slaves of all ages into the college chapel from the neighboring plantations, by the permission of their masters, for a Sunday-school. The second year of my college life I was invited to superintend a colored Sunday-school, taught by benevolent white people in the city, numbering about five hundred of all ages. This school I continued to superintend as long as I stayed in Washington. My first vacation I spent by invitation in the family of a planter in the vicinity of the college, and held religious services in a deserted Episcopal house of worship in the neighborhood. I conducted these in my own way, and had for my hearers the families of neighboring planters and some genteel families from the city who were residing in the country. I was occasionally invited to their houses to dine. My congregation was facetiously called by some of my fellow-students my 'flock of goats.'"

In addition to these labors in the cause of Christ, while he was a student, Mr. Thresher spent his second summer vacation in a tour on horse-back, for his health, in the upper counties of Virginia, among the Baptist churches of that region, in company with his fellow-student, Baron Stow. The following letter from Dr. Stow, written nearly thirty years afterward, will be of interest:

"BOSTON, 24 March, 1855.
"MY DEAR BROTHER:

"Pardon me if I presume a little on the basis of old friendship, and write more to gratify myself than to benefit you. The older I grow the more my heart reverts to the dear friends of my former days and finds pleasure in recollecting the scenes with which we were jointly familiar.

"Laid aside from labor by the loss of my voice, I have been perusing my journal of thirty years ago. Under date of February 16, 1825, I find a record of your first visit, by my introduction, to the Fenner family. Do you remember it? Of course you do, for 'thereby hangs a tale.' My record says that Miss Fenner and Miss Eliza were at that time deeply serious, inquiring the way of eternal life. Oh, how fresh is my recollection of that evening spent in what I regarded as the most religious family that I knew in Washington!

"On the 28th of April following you and I started for Upperville, Virginia. We stopped the first night at Mr. Hixson's, Dover Mills. At Upperville we found a home at Dr. Smith's. On the Sabbath you preached, and I preached, and old Father Latham preached, in the old barn-like meeting-house in the oak grove. The next day, with Dr. Smith, his son Adolphus, Mr. Wright, and Mr. Wilkinson, we started for Harper's Ferry, passing through the Blue Ridge by Snicker's Gap and the Devil's Race-ground, and thence down by Shanondale Springs, along that beautiful valley of the Shenandoah. You remember how we carved our names on Jefferson's Rock at Harper's Ferry, and how we attended the monthly concert of prayer in the evening, and what wonders of nature and art we visited the next morning, and how, on our homeward way, we parted from our associates at Hillsboro, and proceeded down to Swann's farm and passed the night with Charles F. Wood, and breakfasted on Wednesday with that antinomian old hunker, Elder Gilmore, at Leesburg, and, passing by the Potomac Falls, reached College Hill in the evening. "O my brother, how little we then anticipated what we have since witnessed and felt! We were then young; now we are growing old. How many the changes in thirty years! Do you wish to return and begin anew? I do not. I have lived very imperfectly, but I have no confidence that if the experiment were allowed, I should live better. God has been good to me, and his continued grace is my only hope. * * * * * *.

"With affectionate esteem,

"Your friend and brother,

"BARON STOW."

In 1826 Columbian College fell into great financial embarrassments, and its students felt compelled to seek admission into other institutions. Mr. Thresher, for this reason, applied for entrance into the junior class of Brown University in Providence, Rhode Island, where he was received in June, 1826. A certificate given him at this time by the Education Committee of the Board of the General Convention, under the auspices of which Columbian College had been conducted, says: "We certify that the whole conduct of Mr. Thresher while at the college has been, to the best of our knowledge, highly exemplary and worthy of universal approbation." This is signed by Luther Rice and by Dr. O. B. Brown, who was for more than forty years pastor of the First Baptist Church in Washington. In this connection also we may quote from some recently written reminiscences by Dr. Robert Ryland. "I was thrown," he says, "into close intimacy with Mr. Thresher at Columbian College. His entire college life was one of industry, fidelity, and usefulness. He impressed my mind very distinctly as more placid in temper, more conciliatory in manners, more used to society, and better prepared for college than the average student. I loved him at once for his accessible, sincere, ingenuous, and transparent nature. And all my study of his character since has only intensified my love into admiration. As he was in the class below me, I could form no definite idea of his scholarship. But in his chapel declamations and in his Enosinian speeches I was struck with his clear voice, his distinct enunciation, and his earnest manner, and predicted for him a brilliant career as a pulpit orator. How grieved was I afterward to learn that *aphonia* had closed his pulpit efforts forever!" For the writer of these fondly appreciative words Mr. Thresher always cherished the highest esteem, and took great delight, a few years before his death, in receiving a visit from him, when they reviewed together the memories of their college days. "Your conversion while in college," he afterward, in 1882, wrote to Dr. Ryland, "drew you very near to us, and nothing has ever occurred in our long lives to sever or even to weaken those ties. Very just is your appreciation of Pratt. He was a true man and a devoted Christian. It has long been my happiness to meet him once a year, and if I shall be permitted to go up to Granville again I shall miss his venerable form and hearty greetings. Thomas Powell died about one year ago in Illinois. He was an eminently useful minister of the gospel and died much respected and lamented. Only three of the college-mates—as far as I am informed—remain, you and Joseph T. Robert and myself."

Mr. Thresher's transfer to Brown University brought him into relations with another group of leading men. His path in life seems to have been ordered so as to give him an unusually large and valuable acquaintance. Dr. Messer was at that time the president, but he resigned at the close of that summer term. Rev. Francis Wayland was called to succeed him from the pastorate of the First Baptist Church in Boston. Mr. Thresher graduated in 1827, a member of the first senior class which enjoyed Dr. Wayland's instructions and went forth to their work in life with his benediction. Messrs. De Wolf, Parsons, Woods, Bowen, Goddard, and Elton were professors whose teaching gave character and reputation to the college. Dr. Stephen Gano still ministered to the old First Baptist Church in Providence, but was approaching the end of his long pastorate of thirty-six years. Among those who were Mr. Thresher's fellow-students at Brown, may be mentioned Gov. John H. Clifford of Massachusetts, Dr. John Pratt, and Hon. Charles Thurber, who were his classmates, and Gov. Samuel Coney of Maine, Gov. Elisha Dyer of Rhode Island, Dr.

George I. Chace, and Hon. B. F. Thomas, judge of the Supreme Court of Massachusetts, who were in the classes below him. In a letter written to his brother, near the close of his college course, he speaks of being absent from Providence five weeks, during which he made a trip to Schenectady and West Point. "I was delighted," he says, "with my visit to West Point. I was with very agreeable company, and we were all partially acquainted with Prof. McIlvaine, who had formerly resided in Georgetown, District of Columbia, and who received us very politely." This trip was taken, he says, in consequence of his being in poor health. There are other indications in his memoranda of interruptions and hinderances from poor health during his studies, although he lived so long. The Prof. McIlvaine, to whom he refers, afterward became the well-known bishop of that name in the Episcopal Church.

"The day of my graduation," he says, "formed an important crisis in my life. I had now entered upon the thirtieth year of my age I had already chosen my profession. I had a desire for a full course in a theological institution, but considering my age and the long time I had been anticipating the active duties of the ministry, I concluded to remain one year as a post-graduate, under the instruction of Dr. Wayland, and then do the best I could with what attainments I might have. My pecuniary necessities also influenced me in my decision. I had devoted more than eight

years to study and had expended, in addition to the
small amount of my previous earnings, five hundred
and fifty-five dollars. Of this, two hundred dollars had
come from my brother, fifty from an unknown friend,
ninety-six from the Education Committee of the Baptist Triennial Convention, and two hundred and nine
from the American Education Society, which Rev. Elias
Cornelius, the secretary, had kindly proffered me. The
amounts from my brother and from the American Education Society I considered as borrowed and as within
my reach to return. I paid them as soon as I was able,
with interest. The other amounts I regarded as im-
posing on me a still more sacred obligation to dis-
charge as opportunity might offer."

A few days after his graduation Mr. Thresher was
married to Miss Elizabeth Fenner. Born in Canterbury,
England, and bereaved of her mother in infancy, she
and her older sister had been brought by their father to
this country when she was three years old. They then
settled near Poughkeepsie, New York. The father died
soon after, leaving his young daughters provided with
means of support, but among comparative strangers.
They were kindly received into a family of Friends by
the name of Draper, who were without children, who
tenderly cared for them and whose memory was affectionately cherished by them through life. They became
members of the Dutch Reformed Church in Poughkeepsie, then under the pastoral care of Rev. Dr. Cuyler,

who afterward became pastor of the First Presbyterian Church in Philadelphia. They were residing in Washington with their brother, who was acting as chaplain in the United States Navy Yard, when Mr. Thresher first made their acquaintance. He was then a student in Columbian College, and Miss Fenner was one of the teachers in a colored mission-school, of which he was the superintendent. She became engaged to him when she was on a visit to friends in Providence in the summer of 1826. She was probably one of that "very agreeable company" with whom he made his trip to West Point. Their marriage took place in the city of New York on the thirteenth day of September, 1827. Either before or soon after her marriage, Mrs. Thresher became a member of the Baptist Church, and heartily joined her husband in the chosen work of his life. Miss Sarah Fenner never married, but after twice visiting England, and spending some years there each time with an aged aunt, made her home in the family of her sister, Mrs. Thresher, and afterward in that of her niece, Mrs. Charles H. Crawford, and lived to an advanced age, surviving her sister, and affectionately known for "the good works and alms-deeds which she did."

"While a student in Brown University," says Mr. Thresher, "I superintended the Sunday-school in the First Baptist Church in Providence. While a postgraduate student with Dr. Wayland I taught a Bible-class

4

of married ladies. We met on a week-day afternoon or evening at the houses of the members in rotation. As the class was composed of ladies of intelligence, the exercise became one of great profit to me as well as of pleasure. While with Dr Wayland, I had another opportunity for usefulness which has afforded me pleasant recollections. Deacon Levi Peirce, residing at Middleborough Four Corners, a center of a somewhat numerous population, three or four miles distant from any place of worship, built at his own expense an academy which became a prosperous school, and the building was occupied occasionally for a number of years, evenings or Sundays, as a place of worship. After a few years, Deacon Peirce became impressed with a sense of his duty to build a meeting-house, with a view of collecting a Sunday-school and also a Baptist church, if Providence should favor. This he completed in 1828, and invited me and my wife to come and spend a few weeks in his family, that I might labor with him in gathering and organizing the Sunday-school. We spent the week-days in visiting the families in the surrounding country and inviting all the children to come to the school to be held on Sundays in the new meeting-house, then about completed. On the appointed day the school was organized, consisting of one hundred and thirty scholars, the sight of whom so overcame their generous patron that he wept and sobbed like a child. The following Sabbath the new meeting-house was to be dedicated. A minister from Boston was expected to preach, but for some cause failed to meet his appointment, and the duty fell upon me, which was a great trial. A large concourse of people had assembled, filling the house to its utmost capacity. I did the best I could, and to my surprise the people gave me their undivided attention, which greatly assisted me. In our visits inviting children to the Sunday-school we looked up members of Baptist churches residing in the different neighborhoods. The result was that soon after the organization of the Sunday-school a Baptist church was instituted, which has been a prosperous one to this day."

Peirce Academy, which has become such a well-known and useful institution, afterward passed into the hands of trustees. An act of incorporation had been obtained for this purpose from the legislature of Massachusetts in 1835.

In the autumn of 1828 Mr. Thresher accepted a call to become the pastor of the First Baptist Church in Portland, Maine, at that time the only Baptist church in that city. The call is signed by Alford Richardson in behalf of the church, and by Joseph Noble in behalf of the society. His salary was fixed at seven hundred and fifty dollars, and the expenses of his moving were provided. He had been licensed to preach by the church in Stafford, Connecticut, in 1823. He was ordained in Portland on December 18th, 1828. Dr. Daniel

Sharp, of Boston, preached the sermon from Ecclesi-
astes 12: 10—"*The preacher sought to find out acceptable
words.*" Other important parts in the services, as as-
signed by the council, were the ordaining prayer by
Rev. David Nutter, of Livermore, and the giving of the
hand of fellowship by Rev. Alonzo King, of North
Yarmouth. Both of these names have been fragrant
in the memory of those who knew them. The latter
was the author of the Memoir of George Dana Boardman. It was especially gratifying to Mr. Thresher that
the address to the church and society could be made
by his college friend, Rev. Baron Stow, who had recently settled at Portsmouth, New Hampshire. The
charge to the candidate was given by Rev. John Butler,
of Winthrop In his old age this faithful minister
came to Ohio and died at the home of his son, Mr.
Charles Butler, of Franklin. Mr. Thresher was one of
the pall-bearers at his funeral. The sermon by Dr.
Sharp, together with the other addresses at the ordina-
ation, was afterward printed by request. The old pam-
phlet is an interesting memorial of good men, who met
on earth in their Master's service, but who have now
entered into his presence above.

Concerning his brief pastorate in Portland, which was
his only one, Mr. Thresher modestly says: "It does
not seem to me to have been attended by any marked
success. I was permitted to baptize as the fruit of
my ministry only ten persons. In some other respects

I think the church had some visible and permanent
growth. I succeeded in establishing, by contributing
largely myself, a tract society, which was much needed
at that early day. I organized a Bible-class, which I
taught on a week-day evening, and which bore some
excellent fruit in after-years. The wife of Rev. Samuel B. Swaim, a lady of devout piety, was a member
of that class. My immediate successor, Rev. George
Leonard, whose pastorate was very short, was blessed
with a powerful revival of religion, as the fruit of
which more than forty were added to the Church.
I have cherished the hope that my ministry may have
contributed a little, by way of preparation, to this
visitation of the Spirit. While pastor in Portland I
labored under some serious embarrassments. I was in-
differently prepared for the work. My limited course
of education was chiefly elementary, and, although it
gave me a good foundation for professional studies,
few attainments had as yet been made. Commencing
my education so late in life I not only had everything to learn but much to unlearn. I had many de-
mands on my time, and was a member of the school-
committee of Portland. I found also that my voice
was extremely feeble. The older members of my congregation complained that they could not hear me.
By too constant application to books and a neglect,
in my ignorance, of the laws of health, I had broken
down in my freshman year in college and had not

since fully recovered my muscular strength. I was told before going to Portland that I would find the church a difficult one to please. This caused me some anxiety; but I realized no particular difficulty from this source. The church was always courteous to me as their pastor and exceedingly kind to me and my family. My predecessor was settled when a mere youth, and being very amiable in disposition had conceded many things, which belonged to him as pastor, to the older members of the church. I found in the church when I came some discordant elements. A few of the older members entertained extreme views on the subject of discipline. One expressed to me his opinion that the church was in a bad way, that there ought to be more frequent meetings for discipline as had been the custom formerly, when, if a brother passed another on the street without speaking, or if a sister wore ribbons on her bonnet, a church-meeting was called to put them under discipline.

"My greatest trial in Portland, which consumed my time and drank up my spirit, was sickness in my family. My wife was very ill for a whole year, and the rigorous climate of Portland had begun to make serious inroads upon my own health, inducing disease of the throat and lungs. I became satisfied, after a residence there of fifteen months, that it was my duty to resign and move away. If I had desired, the people would have granted me leave of absence; but I felt satisfied the church needed the active services of a pastor, and should choose one as soon as possible. Having begged the deacons and the leading members of the church to comply with my decision, I offered my resignation on Sunday, the 14th of March, 1830. At my request the church met on the following evening, and voted to accept it. On Saturday of the same week I left Portland with my family."

In his diary we find the following entries made at this time:

"*March* 20.—I leave my friends in tears and in great distress. May the Good Shepherd preserve and bless these lambs of his flock! This is a trying day to me.

"*March* 21.—We journeyed yesterday as far as Portsmouth, New Hampshire, and have spent the Sabbath with my old and dear friend, Baron Stow. The Lord is pouring out his Spirit on him and on his people. I tried to preach once for him, but found my lungs very weak.

"*March* 22.—Journeyed as far as Salem. Lodged with Brother Babcock."

This was Rev. Rufus Babcock, who had been a tutor at Columbian College and was now pastor of the Baptist Church in Salem. He afterward became president of Waterville College. The diary continues:

"*March* 26, CHARLESTOWN, MASSACHUSETTS.—We find ourselves by no means improved by traveling. The babe is almost sick. My wife is worse, and I am

taken violently ill with a fever. This is now the third
day I have been confined to my room. Through a
kind and gracious Providence I am better. Have been
much distressed both in mind and body, and am sensible of great sinfulness. I am much perplexed about
my future course. Lord, give me repentance for my
sins and guide me by thy Spirit! These are memora-
ble days, days of trial. May God, my heavenly Father,
graciously sanctify them to me and enable me to adore
his goodness! Amen."

On the 5th of April he was so far recovered that he
"preached in the morning for Brother Jackson, in the
afternoon heard Brother Knowles, and in the evening
preached for Brother Weston." In the following week he
journeyed to Providence, where he attended the Rhode
Island Baptist Convention. Thence, having found a
temporary home for his infant daughter among friends,
he started with his wife on a journey for their health,
visiting New York, Philadelphia, Baltimore, and Washington. In Washington he mentions preaching "at the
Navy Yard for Brother Rollin H. Neale," who was then
a senior in Columbian College, but who afterward became so widely and long known as pastor of the First
Baptist Church of Boston. He also speaks of seeing
for the first time Dr. Stephen Chapin, then president
of the college, and characterizes him as "a grave old
gentleman." Under another date he says: "Dr. Semple
left the city for Fredericksburg. The doctor is a plain,

straightforward, common-sense man." On their return to Philadelphia they worshiped at the churches of Drs. Dagg and W. T. Brantly, senior. This trip occupied one month, and was greatly beneficial to both invalids. Returning to Providence, Mr. Thresher heard Dr. Wayland preach the sermon at the ordination of Messrs. E. A. Crawley and John Pryor, (both afterward presidents of Acadia College, Nova Scotia,) and in Boston, on the following Sunday, after preaching for Rev. J. D. Knowles in the Baldwin Place Church in the morning, he witnessed in the evening the setting apart of Messrs. Francis Mason and Eugenio Kincaid, with their wives, as missionaries to Burmah

Three days later, on the 26th of May, 1830, he was elected corresponding secretary of the Northern Baptist Education Society. This had grown out of the Massachusetts Baptist Education Society, which had been formed in 1814* by Rev. Messrs. Sharp, Baldwin, Bolles, Chaplin, Batchelder and others, which at first had assisted some theological students under Dr. Chaplin at Danvers, Massachusetts, and which afterward had promoted the establishment of Waterville College, Maine, now Colby University, which opened with Dr. Chaplin for its theological teacher in 1818, and of Newton Theological Institution, which opened in 1825. The necessity had now become apparent of so changing the

---

*The year of the first Baptist General Convention. Many kindling sparks were blown from that fire.

5

form of that society that it might derive means of support from all the northern states, even as it received
beneficiaries from all. The act of incorporation for the
new society bears date March 5th, 1830, and mentions
the names of Daniel Sharp, Lucius Bolles, Ebenezer
Nelson, James D. Knowles, Bela Jacobs, Cyrus P. Gros-
venor, Howard Malcom, Henry Jackson, and John B.
Jones as corporators. The first annual meeting, at
which Mr. Thresher was elected corresponding secretary,
occurred in Boston at the Federal Street Baptist meeting-house. The active participants were Rev. Lucius
Bolles, D. D., Rev. E. Nelson, the secretary of the former
society, Rev· John O. Chowles of Newport, Rev. Mr.
Chase of Vermont, Prof. H. J Ripley of Newton, Rev.
J. D. Knowles of Boston, Rev. Mr. Going of Worcester,
and Rev. Henry Jackson of Charlestown. Dr. Bolles,
who was the corresponding secretary for the Baptist
Foreign Missions, a position for which he had been
prepared by his twenty-two years' pastorate at Salem,
and his intimate connection with the beginnings of
that movement, was also elected president of this organization. He was succeeded the following year by
Dr. Sharp. Rev. Bela Jacobs of Cambridge was the
first vice-president, Rev. Henry Jackson of Charlestown secretary, and Mr. John B. Jones treasurer. In
the list of the first life-members we find the names
of such noble laymen as Jonathan Bacheller, Ensign
Lincoln, Nathaniel R. Cobb, Levi Farwell, and Nicholas

Brown,—names forever inseparable from the history of our denomination in New England. The new society began with fifty-seven beneficiaries, to be supported at an annual expense of four thousand two hundred and seventy-five dollars. Its object, which it still pursues, was "to aid, in acquiring a suitable education, such indigent pious young men of the Baptist denomination as shall give satisfactory evidence to the churches of which they are members, that they are called of God to the Gospel ministry."

Mr. Thresher says: "The conviction that I must give up, on account of my ill health, the hope of spending my life in pastoral service was the overturning of all my long-cherished plans, the relinquishment of a service which I consider the most desirable and the most exalted with which a mortal can be intrusted. I cheerfully accepted the appointment of the Education Society as near akin to the pastorate, inasmuch as it would prepare others more acceptably to preach the Gospel. The work was left chiefly to my own discretion. The primary object of my appointment was to seek out young men having a conviction of duty to preach the Gospel, and to aid such as needed assistance; but I found it necessary also to enter into many plans for the encouragement of good learning in the Baptist denomination. At that time comparatively few of our ministers had enjoyed a collegiate education; still fewer a theological one. Prejudices and false sentiments hindered some who would otherwise have sought more instruction. Pedobaptists had attached too much importance, for that early day, to learning in the ministry; and persecution had led Baptists to dislike most everything which was characteristic of their persecutors. Wrong views also existed as to a call to the ministry, some thinking that such a conviction must be opposed until it becomes altogether irresistible. Some, too, entertained the false notion that if a man were called to preach he would be divinely assisted, when the occasion came, without any preparation on his part. This state of things required great prudence on the part of the friends of education, lest they should be misunderstood and excite hurtful opposition to their cause. There was, however, now a pretty strong current in favor of ministerial education; and among those who favored it, to their honor be it spoken, there were not a few who had entered the ministry themselves without any special literary preparation. Some of these had risen to prominence, and were the friends of learning because they had felt the need of it."

Mr. Thresher threw himself into his work with great zeal. He traveled among the Baptist churches of New England, advocating the cause in public and private. As a preacher he had few of what are called popular gifts, but was thoughtful and earnest; and in personal conversation he acquired a strong influence over many minds, stirring them up to the importance of Christian culture. His journeys, of course, had to be made chiefly by stage or carriage. He was found at the various state conventions and associations, making his appeals, forming local educational societies, securing scholarships and life memberships, and hunting out thoughtful young men into whose minds he dropped the seeds of nobler ambitions. The following entries in his diary the first year give us glimpses of his work:

"*June* 1.—Rode to Pomfret. Called on Deacon ———. He says ministers are getting too much power; that no man will preach for them short of a thousand dollars if things go on in this way; that the New Testament does not require us to educate ministers.

"*June* 3.—Attended the Ashford Association, held in Willington. Found four young men in this association who are hopeful candidates for the ministry.

"*June* 8.—Met with the Baptist Education Society of Connecticut. The society is full, with four young men under its patronage. Was formed in 1814.*

"*June* 22.—Left Boston for New Hampshire. Passed through Lowell, Nashua, Amherst, Claremont.

"*June* 24.—Attended the convention; formed an education society. On Thursday went to Windsor and made Leland Howard a life member.

"*June* 30.—Arrived home at Providence.

"*July* 3.—Made Thomas P. Ives a life member of the society.

---

*The year of the first Baptist General Convention.

"*July* 5. — Constituted the first scholarship in Providence called scholarship No. 1. May it become one of fifty formed in 1830. O Lord, dispose the hearts of many to this good work!

"*July* 30. — Brother Jones ordained a missionary to the heathen, in Brother Malcom's meeting-house, Federal Street, Boston.

"*October* 3. — Preached in Portsmouth and baptized two persons.

"*December* 5. — Baptized for Dr. Sharp five persons.

"*January* 9. — Preached once for Brother Malcom.

"*January* 19. — Obtained five annual subscribers."

The annual meetings of the society became occasions of special interest, when not only were the reports read but addresses were made by prominent ministers and educators. The secretary improved these occasions to discuss the work and enforce its claims. In his first report, 1831, he announced that societies for the same object which had previously existed, or had been formed with his advice during the year in other New England states, had become branches. The arrangement was that if any branch had more funds than beneficiaries, or more applicants for aid than funds, the excess in each case should be turned over to the parent society. He also used the following language: "It is not unfrequently the case that a young man cherishes a desire to devote his life to the Gospel ministry for years without revealing his secret to any one. Such may be his indigence and obscurity that, though possessed of the genius and piety of a Bunyan, he would subject himself to ridicule were he to declare his conviction of duty. *Such are the men whom this Society proposes to adopt as her children.* She calls to them in the language of the omnipotent Savior to the entombed Lazarus, 'Come forth.' Suppose they should commence an education with their scanty means, determined to acquire it by their industry, as hundreds have done, what a considerable portion of their best days by this slow process would be lost to the Church! The labors of this society have already saved, unquestionably, to the Church many years of valuable ministerial labor."

By the end of his second year of work, 1832, he could say, "The past year has been one of great success. The number of young men who have consecrated their lives to the ministry, and are now in a course of education under the patronage of this society, has been nearly doubled. One hundred and twenty-nine have been assisted. It has also been ascertained that there are in New England three hundred Baptist young men pursuing a course of study preparatory to the ministry. The ordinary receipts of the past year exceed the receipts of the preceding year by one thousand and twenty-two dollars and twenty-seven cents. In several associations there are provisions for receiving contributions. The various female education societies in different parts of the country form a powerful auxiliary.

We place great reliance also on young men's education societies. The Young Men's Education Society of Boston has resolved to support during the current year six young men "

In 1833 he reports one hundred and thirty-eight beneficiaries assisted by the society and its branches, and says: "We believe it quite possible for a man to live and die in neglect of his duty to preach the Gospel. We believe means are employed by this society eminently calculated to arouse such from their slumbers. To assist in acquiring an education any indigent young man of correct moral principle is a benefaction of a high order; but when we consider that this benefaction is to be bestowed upon an individual of undoubted piety, who gives evidence moreover that God has made it his duty to preach the Gospel, the importance of the act becomes exceedingly magnified; because he is to be exclusively employed in dispensing the richest favors which heaven has to bestow on a fallen world." In the same report he calls attention to the cheering fact that, within the two years preceding, funds to a considerable amount had been raised by the friends of education toward the establishment of academies in different parts of New England; for one in Brandon, Vermont, seventeen thousand dollars; for one in Suffield, Connecticut, ten thousand dollars; for one in Franklin County, Massachusetts, five thousand dollars; and for one in Worcester County, Massachusetts, five thousand dollars. "They are all," he says, "to a certain extent on the manual labor system, and have been established, though not exclusively for this purpose, yet with special reference to the education of young men for the Christian ministry. The success of our colleges and of Newton Theological Institution will very much depend upon the increase and good regulations of these preparatory schools."

It was also in 1833 that he issued a "Pastoral Letter to the Beneficiaries," from the thoughtful sayings of which we take the following: "The board do not regard the annuity which you receive as a charity. Charity is the bestowment of favors upon the children of misfortune for which no equivalent is expected. Neither of these elements enter into your case."—"If you should at any time find yourselves declining in grace, leave all for the moment that you may recover yourselves, and come back to the path. Do not flatter yourselves that it is enough for the present that you are scholars, supposing that by and by the duties of your profession will possess sufficient influence to regulate the heart!"— "It would seem an impeachment of infinite wisdom to suppose that a faculty of such astonishing powers and capable of such unlimited improvement as the human intellect, could not be exercised without breaking down that tenement that is fitted up for its accommodation. If a student would preserve his health he has only to take heed to those laws which Heaven has es-

6

tablished and which every one has the means of knowing."—"A good education consists not so much in a
knowledge of facts as in the attainment of intellectual
stature. Learn to think, and think for yourselves."—
"While I would dissuade you from frequent attempts
at preaching in the early stages of your education, I
would apply to each of you with solemn emphasis the
exhortation of the apostle to Timothy, 'Neglect not
the gift that is in thee.' Habituate yourselves to efforts
to do good. Cultivate early a habit of extemporaneous
speaking on religious topics."—"Pay due attention to
personal appearance. There should be no semblance of
foppishness or pride; but gentility, ease, and affability
are perfectly compatible with that meekness and sim-
plicity of character which ought to appear in a minister of Christ."—"No man in his senses would suppose
that a few pounds of small iron could be thrown with
sufficient force to demolish the strong wall of a fortifi-
cation; but then, let this little budget be employed in
spiking the guns, and it might be sufficient to render
powerless a range of artillery of the requisite force to lay
the whole defense prostrate. I would say, then, study
to be strictly accurate in everything."—"The funda-
mental principle of the Reformation is that the Word of
God as revealed from heaven, in its exact proportions,
and unadulterated with human creeds, is the only rule
of Christian faith and practice. To maintain our high
position as a denomination will require that we know

what the Bible teaches and what it does not teach, and it becomes us to advance to the contest with well-practiced weapons; a contest not for the mastery, but for the truth."—"I would have you at the same time cherish toward all Christians of other denominations the most affectionate regards." These fragmentary extracts may serve to illustrate the spirit of his counsels, which was also the spirit of the man.

In May, 1834, he mentions that "the school in Suffield, Connecticut, commenced instruction in August. The school in Brandon, Vermont, went into operation in March. The high-school in Worcester, Massachusetts, will be opened the 4th of June." In regard to the relation of such institutions to the state, he says: "Liberty to possess and use the requisite funds as voluntary associations is all the protection to literary institutions we could ask for from legislators, because it is all the protection, as we believe, that can be of any service to them or to the interests of education as connected with them."

The beneficiary work continued to prosper until in May, 1837, the society and its branches had one hundred and eighty-six young men receiving assistance. For the three years previous to this a financial secretary, Rev. E. Nelson, had also been employed, and had greatly helped on the work. The greatest annual expenditure by the society and its branches was in the year ending in May, 1836; namely, ten thousand two

hundred and fifty-four dollars and ninety-two cents.
Then came years of financial depression in the country,
when most benevolent enterprises suffered. It is worthy
of note, as the testimony of some experience on a question that frequently arises, that in 1833 the society
adopted the rule of requiring beneficiaries to give their
notes, and thus of regarding the amounts furnished to
them as loans. In 1843 it was voted that serving three
years in the ministry after completing a course of education should cancel a student's note. In 1844 it was
determined to abandon the note system entirely. Mr.
Thresher continued in office through that year. It is
evident that his labors had been extremely useful. It is
true that when he began the time was ripe for the
movement, and that all through his term of service he
had the counsel, co-operation, and support of several
prominent ministers, and of such laymen as Levi Farwell, Ensign Lincoln, Heman Lincoln, and Nathaniel R.
Cobb. Levi Farwell was deacon of the First Baptist
Church in Cambridge, and for many years the "steward"
of Harvard University. Important civil trusts were com-
mitted to his hands. "He was," says Dr. H. J. Ripley,
"a man of sound judgment and an example of pure
and consistent piety. He and his wife can never cease
to be held in the kindest remembrance." Ensign Lincoln was the head of the publishing house of Lincoln
and Edmands, but often exercised his gifts by preaching
to feeble Baptist churches in the vicinity of Boston.

Dr. Wayland said of him: "You may look over a dozen cities before you find a man in a private station who has cleared away around him so large and so fertile a field of usefulness." Heman Lincoln served in the legislature of Massachusetts, and was the first president of the American Baptist Home Mission Society (of which Jonathan Going may be regarded as the founder and John M. Peck as the forerunner). He was also one of the first promoters of Baptist foreign missions, for twenty-two years chairman of the Executive Committee, and the constant entertainer of missionaries in his hospitable home in Boston. It has been said that "the cause of Christ was dearer to him than personal reputation or any earthly good." Nathaniel R. Cobb was a young and successful merchant. To his last days Mr. Thresher cherished the fondest recollections of these and other fellow-laborers, and spoke with deep tenderness of his last interview with Mr. Cobb, ("our great patron," as he calls him in the annual report which mentions his death,) when the latter was confined to his room by his last illness and gave expression, in conversation with his visitor, to his anticipations of heaven. Mr. Cobb was born the same year with Mr. Thresher. His remarkable generosity has often been referred to, but a brief mention of it here may not be out of place. When he was twenty-three years old he signed his name to the following resolution: "By the grace of God, I will never be worth over fifty thousand dollars. By the

grace of God, I will give one fourth of the net profits
of my business to charitable and religious uses. If I
am ever worth twenty thousand dollars I will give one
half of my net profits; and if I am ever worth thirty
thousand dollars I will give three fourths; and the
whole after fifty thousand. So help me God, or give
to a more faithful steward, and set me aside." It is
said that he entered business at twenty-one a thousand
dollars in debt, and died at the age of thirty-six, supposing himself to be worth fifty thousand dollars, and
having given away forty thousand dollars. This was a
very large amount for those days. Not only the Education Society but Newton Theological Institution, and
many other objects, enjoyed his generosity. His example had a great influence on other minds, and Mr.
Thresher often took pleasure in referring to it in later
years. But while he had such excellent helpers, to Mr.
Thresher's untiring efforts must be given a large part of
the credit of what was accomplished. His largest salary
in the service of the society was eight hundred dollars.
A portion of the time it was less, and one year he
served gratuitously.

His own experience had fitted him to seek out young
men contending with poverty and to sympathize with
them most deeply. When in the list of those with
whom he was thus brought into relation as an adviser
we find the names of such honored workers at home or
abroad as Sewell S. Cutting, Josiah Goddard, Dura D.

Pratt, Joseph G. Binney, Samuel B. Swaim, and S. S.
Greene among those who have died, and among those
who are still living several widely known in the denomination as successful pastors, missionaries, or educators,
we are impressed by the wide range of his influence and
of the value of the investments which the society at his
suggestions made. One at the head of an important institution wrote to him a year or two before his death:
"My acquaintance with you is of longer standing than
that with any other living man. I met you the first
morning I arrived in Boston. I was then in rather a
sad plight. I had had a rough passage by sea, and had
taken cold. I knew nobody and had little money. I
was a stranger and you took me in. As long as I was
a student I found a welcome at your house. I often
wonder why such an adventurer should meet with so
much kindness at the hands of such persons as your-
self, Dr. and Mrs. Sharp, Prof. Ripley, and President
Wayland. I trust you have not forgotton how to beg.
If you had not been somewhat skilled in that not very
agreeable business I should not have been here; for
without help I never could have obtained the little
knowledge I have acquired." Another, now among the
oldest and best esteemed Baptist ministers in Ohio,
writes: "I knew him in my childhood days. I was
encouraged by him to preach Christ's Gospel. In my
early ministry in Massachusetts he was my friend
and counselor." Much more such testimony might be

gathered. In view of the decrease in the number of students for the ministry in proportion to the enlargement of the denomination, the question arises whether more such personal service as Mr. Thresher rendered ought not now to be employed. Is there not too great a disposition to wait for candidates to offer themselves for the ministry instead of seeking out suitable ones and suggesting to them a course of education for this purpose? In one of his published reports he has marked with his pencil a quotation which he ascribes to Martin Luther: "If ever there be any considerable blow given to the kingdom of Satan it must be by well educated young men."

Indeed, he brought forward not only beneficiaries but benefactors. He engaged the sympathy of many who afterward became strong helpers. The Young Men's Baptist Education Society of Boston, which had existed since 1819, as well as similar organizations recently formed in other cities, furnished him valuable opportunities which he was quick to improve. With the encouragement of himself and his co-laborers this society had public meetings in the churches, when sermons and other addresses were delivered by distinguished members of the denomination, and much enthusiasm was manifested. On one such occasion, in the Federal Street meeting-house, when Messrs. Thresher, Knowles, and Stow had spoken, contributions were pledged to the amount of more than one thousand dollars. How many of the young laymen

in our city churches to-day have interest enough in
ministerial education to hold such meetings for its direct promotion? The late Gardner Colby, who was a
member of that young men's society, who was treasurer
of the Education Society from 1839 to 1845, and whose
name is so associated with some of our institutions of
learning, used to say that he owed the beginnings of his
interest in this subject to the appeals of Mr. Thresher.
He referred to the time when he was scarcely out of
his minority and a member of the Baptist church in
Charlestown. He was urged by Mr. Thresher to un-
dertake the collection in that church of one hundred
and fifty dollars, the amount of two scholarships. He
cheerfully accepted the service, and accomplished it on
Thanksgiving day when he was released from the store
where he was employed. He gave five dollars of it
himself, which was a large contribution for him at that
time. He never ceased to hold in the highest esteem
the man who had thus enlisted him in the cause of
education.

Reference has already been made to the fact that Mr.
Thresher's secretaryship in the Northern Baptist Education Society brought him at the same time into other
enterprises promotive of intelligence and strength in the
denomination. He felt it to be his duty to advocate
good learning in every way and was glad to avail himself of the press. In 1831 and 1832 he edited *The American Baptist Magazine*. This periodical, the oldest in the

7

denomination, had been commenced, with the word "Massachusetts" in the place of "American" on its title page, as early as 1803, but since 1826 it had been the organ of the Triennial Convention. Although it afterward became *The Baptist Missionary Magazine*, its contents at the time of which we speak were of quite a miscellaneous character, being largely biographical sketches of distinguished ministers and laymen, essays, reviews, letters, and journals. Mr. Thresher accepted the appointment of editor because, as he said, it gave him an opportunity both to promote the cause of education and to become familiar with our foreign missions. During these years many communications appeared in its pages from Judson, Boardman, Wade, and other early missionaries, which were read with great interest among the churches. Especially may be mentioned Francis Mason's account of the death of Boardman. The editor was allowed to have an educational department, which an examination of the pages shows he well improved. Among other interests in this line, Newton Theological Institution is often advocated. In the number for February, 1832, is a plan for supporting two professorships in the institution by raising a sinking fund of twenty thousand dollars to be expended, principal and interest, in twenty years. Before that, the professors had been supported by annual contributions from churches and individuals. It had been a part of Mr. Thresher's work to beg the necessary amount the previous year, and he had found that it stood greatly in the way of raising the money necessary for the young men who were students The new plan was successfully accomplished, securing a salary of eight hundred dollars to each professorship for a series of years.

He was also editor of *The Christian Watchman* from November, 1834, to December, 1836. Writing many years afterward to the editor of that paper he says: "I had occasionally contributed articles which had introduced me to the favor of Deacon James Loring, who had edited the paper from its origin up to that time. A practical printer, he was also a judicious and able editor, who commanded universal respect. He had now become old and had determined to retire from public service. He was hastened to this conclusion by the feverish condition of the public mind upon the subject of slavery. In the New England states there were two parties, the extreme and the moderate Abolitionists, which antagonized each other sometimes with extreme bitterness, so that it became exceedingly difficult for a fair-minded editor to give satisfaction to either party. Deacon Loring besought me to take his place, which I consented to do, retaining my connection with the Education Society. He withdrew his name as editor November 14, 1834, when my services commenced; but my name did not appear as editor till January, 1836. William Nichols, a practical printer, was both proprietor and publisher of the paper at that time. He was a

worthy but sensitive Christian man, and the care of
the paper in those exciting days proved too much for
his nervous system to bear. The extreme Abolitionists
originated *The Christian Reflector*, which antagonized *The
Watchman*, and became a competitor for the patronage
which was only sufficient then to give a scanty support to one paper. Mr. Nichols was perpetually harassed
with the fear that he was about to lose both his reputation and his small fortune, all of which he had in-
vested in the paper. He became so unhappy that I
proposed to him to purchase it, which I did, paying him
the sum of four thousand dollars, which was thought
to be a fair price. He had become so shattered that
he was obliged to seek rest in seclusion. After a period,
however, he returned to his friends in Boston, who,
hoping that employment at his former business would
then contribute to his restoration, proposed to me to
reconvey the paper to him, which I did, and for the
same price which I had given him for it. I then left
the editorial chair and was succeeded by Rev. William
Crowell. Another cause of public excitement which
gave an editor no little labor in 1836 was the subject
of Bible distribution in heathen lands, a subject sprung
upon the denomination by the vote of the American
Bible Society discriminating against the versions made
by our missionaries. So you see, Mr. Editor, that I was
called upon to navigate a very stormy sea; and I con-
gratulate you on the privilege of sailing on smoother

waters, and yet upon waters, it may be, which require a pretty sharp lookout."

The file of *The Watchman* for that period brings before us the men and scenes of half a century ago. Besides its chronicle of news from the churches, of revivals, dedications, ordinations, and various public meetings, the principal speakers at which have since left noble records, it has strong editorials upon the subjects of education, — always prominent, — Christian benevolence, and the slavery question. It prints the messages of Andrew Jackson, president of the United States, and Edward Everett, governor of Massachusetts. It speaks of various addresses by Drs. Cox and Hoby, a deputation from the English Baptists to their brethren in this country; indorses the personal appeals of President Pratt and Professor Carter in behalf of the young Literary and Theological Institution at Granville, Ohio; deplores the work of the mob which had assailed a meeting held at the rooms of the Anti-slavery Society on Washington Street, and from which William L. Garrison, being the chief speaker, barely escaped with his life; describes the farewell services at the sailing of twenty missionaries at one time, among whom were the Ingalls, the Haswells, the Days, E. L. Abbott, and Miss Macomber, besides other earnest laborers, and who were accompanied by Rev. Howard Malcom on his visit to the mission-stations in Asia; laments the deaths of William Carey, Bela Jacobs, Luther Rice, and Joseph Grafton; and records Dr.

Shurtleff's gift to the college at Alton, Illinois. In regard to the action of the American Bible Society in 1836, above referred to, there are full discussions. The editor shared in the aggrieved feelings of the denomination, but counseled a continuance on the part of Baptists to participate in the home work of that society if possible, suggested that the distribution of the Scriptures in other lands could be made an auxiliary department of our foreign missions, and deprecated the formation of the "American and Foreign Bible Society" by Baptists as hasty if not altogether unnecessary — opinions which he continued to hold without any material modification to the end of his life.

In 1836, after Mr. Thresher's retirement from *The Watchman*, *The Christian Review* was started. *The Baptist Magazine* was thenceforth to be devoted exclusively to missionary subjects, and it was thought by the Baptist Ministerial Conference of Massachusetts a good time for the beginning of a more scholarly periodical in the interests of the denomination. Stock in the enterprise was subscribed for, and an association formed, which appointed an executive committee of five to superintend the work. Ebenezer Thresher is the first name on that committee. Thomas Edmands was made chairman and Caleb Parker secretary. Professor J. D. Knowles of Newton Theological Institution accepted the position of editor. His ability gave it at once a place among the best religious quarterlies. Mr. Thresher took

pains to advocate it in connection with the interests
of education, and letters preserved by him show that
he had an important part in its early affairs. For
twenty-six years it continued to be published under
different editors and to be an able exponent of Baptist
principles, filling the position which *The Baptist Quarterly
Review* now occupies.

Mr. Thresher was a delegate to the Baptist Triennial
Convention in 1835 and onward. The year referred to was
a notable one in the history of our foreign missions.
The Convention met at Richmond, Virginia. He left Boston on Monday afternoon, April 19, in company with his
ministerial brethren, Messrs. Bolles, Stow, Hague, Knowles,
Leverett, Aldrich, and Deacon Heman Lincoln. The
last named, he said in his editorial correspondence to
The Watchman, had given his entire time gratuitously for
the previous five years to the duties of the treasurership
for foreign missions. Proceeding to Providence they em-
barked on a steamboat. Delayed by a fog at Newport they
had religious services on the boat, as also on subsequent
evenings. They arrived in Richmond on Thursday night.
The eloquent Dr. Spencer H. Cone, of New York, was
made president. Great interest was felt in the fraternal
message brought to the Convention by the English deputation. The report of the board dwelt upon two events
of special significance, the completion of the translation
of the Bible into Burmese by Adoniram Judson, and
the baptism of J. G. Oncken and his companions by

Rev. Barnas Sears in Germany. The former fact was
the occasion of profound gratitude. The latter was the
beginning of a work the greatness of which none could
then foresee. It was at the same meeting of the Convention that Rev. Amos Sutton, a missionary of the
General Baptist Missionary Society of England to Orissa
in southern India, was introduced and cordially welcomed. By his appeals the board was induced to send
missionaries that year to the Teloogoos—the first glim-
mer of that "Lone Star" which has now become so
large a constellation. Mr. Thresher was a member of the
Board of Managers of the Convention and of the "Acting Board" (now the "Executive Committee") from 1841
to 1845. He therefore participated in the anxieties and
discussions which agitated the board at that time. The
slavery question was greatly disturbing the co-operation
of the northern and the southern churches in the work.
The unwillingness of the extreme antislavery men in
the denomination to receive into the treasury "the
known avails of slavery" led to the formation by them
in 1840 of a "Provisional Foreign Missionary Committee," and, three years later, of the Baptist Free Mission
Society. These movements, of course, greatly embarassed
the operation of the board in Boston until, in 1845,
the southern Baptists withdrew and formed the Southern
Baptist Convention, and the work at the north was re-
organized under the name of "The American Baptist
Missionary Union" Mr. Thresher continued to have a

part in these exciting cares until near their culmination, when failing health compelled him to resign.

At the same time with the interests just mentioned and those of the Education Society, Newton Theological Institution continued to receive much of his attention. He had been one of its trustees since 1836 ⸳ In November, 1843, the trustees solicited his exclusive services in behalf of the finances of the institution, but the Board of the Education Society were of the opinion that he could serve both causes, which he therefore endeavored to do. In May, 1844, he reported that he had succeeded in obtaining for the library of the institution a subscription of one thousand dollars per annum for five years. A day or two before he made this report, Deacon Levi Farwell, with whom he was very intimate, and who had for many years given his mind and heart to caring for all the affairs of the institution, had died. At the next meeting of the trustees Mr. Thresher was requested to succeed him in the office of treasurer, which was at that time one of peculiar difficulties. There were the buildings, farm, and steward to be looked after, difficulties arising from the boarding of the students in commons to be settled, and the board bills of the students to be regularly collected. The salaries of the professors were inadequate, the property was incumbered with mortgages, and the funds were rapidly decreasing. All this imposed much care and labor on the treasurer. Mr. Thresher's health did not permit him to accept a permanent .election, but he performed the duties for one year, when he was succeeded by Gardner Colby. Thus he added to the very practical and important services already mentioned as rendered by him to the institution in earlier years. He never ceased to cherish a deep interest in it. In this connection it should also be mentioned that he was one of the Board of Trustees of Brown University from 1842 to 1848.

During the time of his connection with these different public interests in New England he had resided at first in Boston, a member of Doctor Sharp's church, and afterward in Roxbury, where he belonged to the Dudley Street Baptist Church, then under the pastoral care of Doctor Caldicott. But he belonged to the cause at large as well as to a particular church; and although he had been early laid aside from the pastorate, we have seen how Providence had overruled this affliction for the wide extension of his ministry. Says Dr. J. N. Murdock: "Few men living or dead have left more beneficent traces on the lines of our denominational life and progress in New England than Ebenezer Thresher. If the present generation of New England Baptists knew him not, it is because the great body of the noble and sainted men with whom he wrought preceded him to the better land."

In the summer of 1845 an entirely new period commenced in Mr. Thresher's life. The scene changed from the East to the West, from the work of the ministry to a secular occupation. His numerous labors had again broken down his health. He had become unable to speak in public on account of the great weakness of his voice, and had grown so feeble that he was thought by his friends to be fast failing with consumption. His physicians expressed grave doubts whether his life could be prolonged a year in the climate of New England, but held out a faint hope that an entire change might be of some benefit. It was therefore to him a season of disappointment and anxiety. For a second time now Providence had apparently closed the path of usefulness he had entered, and he knew not that he could accomplish anything more. Forced to part from many dear friends and associations, and to drop all the responsibilities in which his heart had been so much engaged, he determined to visit Ohio, whither an older brother had gone many years before, and where he had other acquaintances. Hoping almost against hope, he left his family in Roxbury and proceeded on his journey. He seems to have gone to Cincinnati by the way of Baltimore. The railroad was completed as far as Cumberland, Maryland. The route thence was over the mountains by stage to the Ohio river, then by boat to his destination. He had some thought of entering on the culture of fruit as an occupation giving him an opportunity to work in the open air. At Covington, near Cincinnati, he found his friend, Dr. R. E. Pattison, whom he had known in Providence, Rhode Island. After visiting Cincinnati, he was induced for some reason to go to Dayton on the Miami Canal, and as he approached this city he fell into conversation with a congenial fellow-traveler, Mr. Samuel Forrer, who was well known at that time as an engineer of public works, and who resided at Dayton. He thus obtained a favorable idea of the place as one in which to locate. It had been incorporated as a city four years before, and had about ten thousand inhabitants. The hydraulic canal, for water-power purposes, was completed the same year in which Mr. Thresher came. He soon made his arrangements for a prolonged stay, little thinking, however, that he would be spared to have this as his home for more than forty years. He found in the city an earnest and growing Baptist church, then under the pastoral care of Rev. Frederick Snyder, whose ministry is remembered as one of great devotion. Mr. E. E. Barney, whose intellectual culture, as well as his Christian earnestness, had made him a leading member of the church, was the owner at that time of a saw-mill on Wayne Street. He had been a tutor at Granville and the principal of the Dayton Academy, but had been engaged now in this business for three or four years for the recovery of his health. As the Cooper Seminary for young ladies had just been established, and his former success as a teacher had directed the minds of its founders to him as the only suitable man for its principal, he was ready to sell out his mill and lumber business to Mr. Thresher. By this arrangement, to which he was assisted by his wife, Mr. Thresher hoped to give himself the physical and open-air exercise which he felt he most needed. The result was such as to equal his most ardent hopes and to disappoint most happily the fears of his friends. By great prudence together with diligent and cheerful employment he gradually improved, and in two or three years regarded himself as very nearly a well man, though the feebleness of his voice precluded all plans of his again entering the ministry.

When his arrangements and purposes became settled, he left his oldest son, whom he had brought with him, and went east for the rest of his family, who had been boarding during his absence at Newton Center. Meanwhile the canal had been completed between Dayton and Toledo. On the journey westward, therefore, they came by rail as far as Buffalo, thence by steamboat on Lake Erie, and to Dayton by packet on the canal. They stopped for a time at the old Montgomery House, then the principal hotel; but soon they went to housekeeping on Jefferson Street, opposite Market. He felt that his life was now to be in the line of business, and he prosecuted it with great zest, resolved to use whatever prosperity he might gain to further the sacred interests to which at first he had consecrated his strength. He traveled up and down the canal, visiting the forests with ax-men, measuring and buying standing timber,

which he transported to his mill. He also brought to
Dayton a great deal of lumber from Michigan. The
business prospered and increased until the city determined to make a change in the channels for the
water. He then found it necessary to look about for
some better opportunity for business enterprise.

About three years after his coming to Dayton he
found an occasion to call out his old zeal for ministerial
education. It was in the counsels of the Western Baptist Education Society. This society, the organization
of which with the advice of Rev. Jonathan Going in
1834 has already been referred to, had opened, the same
year in which Mr. Thresher came to Ohio, a theological
seminary at Covington, on the south side of the Ohio
river, opposite Cincinnati. Drs. R. E. Pattison and E. G.
Robinson were the professors. But in the very year it
opened occurred the separation of northern and southern
Baptists in their foreign missionary work on account of
slavery, and Dr. Pattison's opinion was at once chal-
lenged by the Baptists of the south-west in regard to
certain decisions of the missionary board at Boston.
Refusing to repudiate those decisions he was denounced
as an Abolitionist, and before long an amendment to the
charter of the institution was passed by the legislature
of Kentucky, putting it into the hands of a new board
of sixteen trustees and giving its control entirely to
men in that state. The Western Baptist Education
Society felt this to be a great injustice, claimed that

there should be at least an equitable division of the
property, and immediately took steps for the establishment of another theological seminary for the north-west.
In the convention which met at Cincinnati in October,
1849, to consider this exciting matter, we find Mr.
Thresher an active participant. When he settled at
Dayton his old friend, Dr. Pattison, had written to him,
expressing regret that he had not decided on Cincinnati as his residence, that they might continue their
intimacy. But he had been near enough to take a deep
interest in what had transpired. He was now brought
into co-operation with Rev. John Stevens, for so many
years before and afterward a leading spirit in all educational movements and the corresponding secretary of the
society, with Rev. John L. Moore, so beloved for his ferv-
ent and self-denying ministry, with Judge A. H. Dun-
levy, Revs. Daniel Bryant, Silas Bailey, O. N. Sage, D. B.
Cheney, Daniel Shepardson, S. B. Page, and others, with
most of whom he afterward labored many years in
building up the cause of Christ in Ohio. A company of
gentlemen had been formed who proposed to purchase
land at Fairmount, near the city, and to donate thirty
acres of it to the society, provided buildings and improvements costing not less than fifteen thousand dollars
were completed within three years, and provided also
the Executive Committee loaned or caused to be loaned
to the company ten thousand dollars for five years. Mr.
Thresher was made chairman of the Committee on Min-

isterial Education, who recommended immediate meas-
ures to raise the sum of fifty thousand dollars. He offered cheerfully to bear his portion of the pecuniary
responsibility. "We must go forward," he said, "and
not backward." After addresses by Rev. Alfred Bennett
and Dr. Nathaniel Colver (who were visitors), Rev. John
Stevens and others, the members of the convention rode
in omnibuses to Fairmount and viewed the site of the
institution their hopes were picturing. Many difficulties, however, beset the enterprise. The men engaged in
it were liberal, but it was hard at that time to raise so
much money. The seminary was opened at last in
a new building in October, 1853, with Rev. Edmund
Turney and Rev. Marsena Stone as professors. It had
seventeen students the first year, and graduated some
efficient ministers. But the plan upon which it was
founded awakened some prejudices, and after a few
years it was obliged to succumb to financial failure. Mr.
Thresher was a member of the Executive Committee of
the Western Baptist Education Society for several years.
Nor did his interest diminish when the work was trans-
ferred, in 1856, to the Ohio Baptist Education Society, of
which he was a firm friend and valued counselor to the
last. He also joined his brethren in the annual gather-
ings of the Dayton Association and Ohio Baptist Convention till the infirmities of age began to increase;
and for some time he participated in the cares of the
quarterly meetings of the Convention board,

About five years after coming to Dayton he purchased of the Cooper estate some land on the north-eastern border of the city, and proposed to Mr. Barney, who was then thinking of retiring from the work of teaching, to form a copartnership for carrying on a manufacturing business. Mr. Barney agreed to the plan. They were not sure at first what they would manufacture, but after Mr. Thresher had made a visit to the East it was decided to make railroad cars. There were then no railroads finished to Dayton; but one connecting the city with Springfield was in process of grading, and there was reason to believe that the future demand for cars would warrant the building of a factory. His old friends in the East had reason to be surprised when he, to whom they had bidden good-by as to an invalid preacher, again appeared among them engaging skilled mechanics to go west to build cars in a place where there was scarcely a railroad. The style of the firm at first was Thresher, Packard & Company. His partner, whose name appeared, had come from the East. Mr. Barney was also a partner from the outset, but it was agreed that at first he should be only a silent one, as the seminary had a claim upon his time for a year longer. At the end of that year his silent partnership became an active one, and about that time, or soon after, Mr. Packard retired. The first building was erected in 1850, Mr. Thresher giving his personal attention to the business. They at first made agricultural imple-

9

ments, and afterward railroad cars. Their capital at the outset was ten thousand dollars. When Mr. Thresher went east for mechanics he brought to Dayton several men who not only proved useful in the business but who afterward became the proprietors of other manufacturing establishments; for example, Messrs. Woodsum, Tenny, Leland, and Tower. The first car built was shipped to its destination on a canal-boat. And the work went on, the retired minister and the retired school-teacher building up a manufacturing interest of prime importance, and showing that their professional labors had not unfitted them for business success. They secured the confidence and esteem of all with whom they had dealings, while their cars became known for the excellence of their material and workmanship. The works thus founded, and at the head of which Mr. Barney continued until his death, have grown into a large establishment of great advantage to the city of Dayton, often employing over twelve hundred men.

Mr. Thresher had been engaged in the car-works, however, only six years when the increase of care again proved too much for his health, and he sold out his interest to Mr. Caleb Parker, whom he had known well as a deacon in the Baptist Church at Roxbury, Massachusetts. Another valuable worker and leader was thus secured for the church in Dayton for many years. Mr. Thresher's name was connected with the business one year afterward. He then permanently retired from it, and, in 1859, associated himself with Mr. Charles F. Tower, who had come from Massachusetts six years before, and with his nephew, Mr. J. B. Thresher, in establishing a manufactory of varnish. He continued in this line of business with a good degree of success until he retired, January 1, 1874, when he was in his seventy-sixth year. So diligent and enterprising was he in these relations that many who had not known his earlier career never imagined that he had not always been a business man. He was careful and strict, plain in his manner of living, shrewd in making bargains, persistent in pursuing his aims, and far-seeing in his discernment of what might be profitable. He was disappointed at one time in his failure to secure the starting of locomotive works at Dayton. Finding that skillful mechanics in that line of work could be secured from the East, he commended the matter to some of his fellow-citizens who had capital. But though a proposition was made and some negotiations took place, no sufficient determination to take hold of the suggestion was developed, and it resulted in nothing.

During the war Dayton was distracted by greatly imbittered parties and witnessed some exciting scenes. The burning of the office of the Republican newspaper by a mob, and the arrest of Vallandigham at night by General Burnside's soldiers took place in the immediate neighborhood of Mr. Thresher's residence, but, while he was earnestly loyal to the Government, he sought no prominence in the conflict. The health of his wife at this time was very poor. She continued for a long while an invalid. Her oldest daughter, Elizabeth, had preceded her to the better world. In August, 1860, she died, leaving two sons and three daughters. To her affectionate sympathy and aid he had been much indebted throughout his career "She was one," said her pastor, Rev. Samson Talbot, "whose intelligence and piety were of the greatest value to the church."

In November, 1861, he was married to Mrs. Martha Snyder. She was the widow of Rev. Frederick Snyder (already mentioned as pastor of the Baptist Church when Mr. Thresher came to Dayton), and was residing in the city with her three children. Her thoughtful and cheerful spirit adapted her to the new relation into which she now entered. For twenty-three years she presided in his home, making it still a scene of attractive Christian hospitality and entering heartily into Christian work.

Mr. Thresher became a trustee of Denison University in 1857. He could not be true to the cause he had early espoused without taking a deep interest in its affairs. In Mr. Barney, also, he found a friend and trustee of the university who was ready to talk with him concerning its field and necessities. A year or two before this, the institution had been removed from the farm to its present beautiful site overlooking the town, and its name had been changed from Granville College.

Rev. Jeremiah Hall, D. D., was then president. A new brick building had been erected, and some funds had been collected; but many difficulties were experienced and the university was running in debt. Soon the war came on, absorbing public attention and depressing all educational enterprises In 1863 its affairs were felt by the trustees to be in a very precarious condition. Rev. Samson Talbot, an alumnus of the institution and the pastor of the Baptist Church in Dayton, was called to the presidency and accepted it with a consecrated spirit. Much self-denying work was before him; but he had noble fellow-laborers in the faculty and was sure of the sympathy and co-operation of some of his leading parishioners in Dayton, and of many other Baptists in the state. Though the property of the university had increased in value in ten years from less than fourteen thousand dollars to about fifty thousand, and though the payment of the debt was provided for, "the faculty were without any visible means of support except the tuition fees of the scanty number of students, and that number was constantly decreasing by enlistment in the army." To meet deficiencies, small contributions began to be asked annually from friends of the university. "Some of you," said the president to the trustees at the annual meeting, "were asked for ten dollars apiece last year; you will be asked for the same this year, and the year following, and so on, until you come to this conclusion: 'It is not the way to do business; let us arise and create a fund for these expenses!' And so each one of these ten-dollar bills has a twofold mission. They meet the expense of instruction, and they become agents on endowment. God speed them on their work!"

In October of the same year, notwithstanding the war was still in progress, the indorsement of the Ohio Baptist Convention was secured to an appeal to the denomination in the state for one hundred thousand dollars to constitute a permanent fund, the income of no part of which should be used until contributions and interest had reached the full amount. The Convention met in Dayton, and the motion prevailed with enthusiasm after Mr. Thresher had made a strong and earnest speech. The month following, President Talbot wrote to him: "The enterprise of an endowment grows in magnitude as I contemplate it. A good college which shall educate the young men of Baptist families, and others not of this fold, will be a process of growth *at the center*, a development without which we can not anticipate anything else than weakness. The meeting at Dayton awakened more than common interest and hope in all parts of the state. We hear of it everywhere. But it will require faith and hard work to get the object before the minds of all the brethren whose help will be needed. What a blessing does money become to him who uses it rightly! He can make his memory sweet in other generations. His example will be worth more

to his children than all his savings. The Baptists of
Ohio are upon trial."

That these words expressed also Mr. Thresher's sentiments is evident from the fact that on the subscription
list his name stands first for ten thousand dollars. It
was one quarter of all he believed himself to be worth
at the time he made the subscription. But this repre-
sents only a part of what he did for the success of the
undertaking. For four years he gave much careful
thought and earnest effort to pushing it on. As he had
been chief in starting the plan he relaxed no effort till
it was completed. He used his voice in pleading for
it in public meetings and in private conversations, and
his pen in many letters and articles for the press. He
never became discouraged. The raising of the endowment was always uppermost in his thoughts till the
work was done. The names of noble and generous co-
workers in the enterprise will come to the minds of
some who read these pages. Mr. Thresher never could
have succeeded without their co-operation, but we think
they all would acknowledge that he was the leading
means under God of raising the institution out of its
condition of poverty and weakness into one of perma-
nence and power. This first substantial addition to its
funds was soon followed by others, in which the late
E. E. Barney, and other generous donors who are still
living, led off. In 1871 another large brick edifice was
erected. Again and again Mr. Thresher's name appears

among the contributors. Before his death he had the
satisfaction of knowing that the university had three
hundred thousand dollars in well-invested funds besides
the lands, two excellent brick buildings and a library
building, the last the generous gift of his friend, Dr.
W. Howard Doane, of Cincinnati. In the meetings of
the trustees he was always present, intensely active in
the discussions till within a year or two of his death.
He carried the university on his heart, commended it
to his brethren whom he expected to live after him,
welcomed to his house only a few days before his departure some of the trustees to talk over plans for its
improvement, and remembered it in his will by a be-
quest of ten thousand dollars for the establishment of
scholarships.

A name so linked with the history of a Christian
college can not easily be forgotten. It is inscribed on
foundation stones on which posterity will build. In a
letter written to him in 1877, Judge T. W. Ewart, of
Marietta, says; "You are, I hope, well aware of the
appreciation of your invaluable services in giving per-
manency to our college in these times which are trying some institutions that have been prosperous in the
past, but are greatly straitened at present for the want
of the wise forecast and liberal planning and labor to
which Granville owes its freedom from embarrassment."
Says Dr. S. B. Page, of Cleveland, who labored for a time
as financial agent of the university, "My acquaintance

81

with him began in 1831 when I was on my way to enter college at Waterville, Maine. I was received kindly and invited to his home in Boston. It was, however, while engaged in the effort to complete the one hundred thousand dollars endowment of our college at Granville, which he so wisely and generously originated and put in motion, that I came to know and more fully appreciate him. I always parted from him with augmented courage and hope. To him more than to any other man must our success be ascribed." Says Dr. E. G. Leonard, of Bucyrus, one of the oldest trustees, "But for Ebenezer Thresher our college might have existed, but it could not have been what it is to-day. Few of the men of this generation can know the extent and value of his influence in this regard. Money he has generously given, but far more than this has been his well-timed counsel and his influence with other noble men whose names are a benediction and a blessing." Dr. William A. Stevens, now of Rochester, writes: "In the work of the college I came to know him intimately. I admired his large wisdom in matters pertaining to the denomination. Our college at Granville, and all who love it, owe him an incalculable debt of gratitude. It was a providential interposition in its history when he was impelled to come to its rescue and identify himself with its great mission." In this connection also we may be permitted to add a few words from one whose name constantly appears with Mr. Thresher's in

10

all the counsels and efforts for the university in its most trying times, Hon. J. M. Hoyt, of Cleveland. In a letter written to his friend in 1883 he says: "That savor of grace which ever pervaded the atmosphere around you, that clear-sighted and ever manly faith which made you a valued leader in enterprises for the furtherance and nurture of righteousness, still have a molding power upon me." And since Mr. Thresher's death he has written: "I shall ponder often, tenderly, joyfully, and instructively upon his inspiring record. I am thankful that I knew and loved him."

In recognition of his greatly useful and long continued services to the cause of education the Board of Trustees of Denison University conferred upon him, in 1875, the honorary degree of Doctor of Laws. He was not a man to think much of titles, but he was not insensible to the appreciation of his brethren. He delighted to meet the Christian men into association with whom his love and labor for the college more or less brought him. It is worthy of note how many of these he survived Samson Talbot, of penetrating intellect and most genial spirit, whose early death he greatly mourned as an almost irreparable loss to the cause, John Stevens, strong in thought and faith and will, Eliam E. Barney, vigorous and broad-minded in business and benevolence, T. W. Ewart, judicial and devout, E. F. Platt, Orsemus Allen, George F. Davis, J. P. Bishop, D. A. Randall, George Cook, and J. W.

King were among these associates who passed away before him.

When the Southern Baptist Theological Seminary was removed from Greenville, South Carolina, to Louisville, Kentucky, in 1877, he began to feel a deeper sympathy with that institution also. This may have been owing in part to the personal interest he had felt in some of its professors ever since they were young men preparing for the ministry. Inducing some of his friends to join with him in the gift, he sent for a few years a considerable sum to aid students at Louisville, and when he found it impracticable to continue this annual effort he made a generous donation to the endowment. He meant this, he said, to express his appreciation, not only of all good learning among our Baptist people and of the work of that institution, but also of fraternal intercommunication between different sections of our great country. He gave it, also, in pleasing recollection of his early intimacy with some southern students for the ministry when he was in Columbian College. Though he could never be called a very wealthy man, his benefactions in private as well as in public were constant and thoughtful. He never gave as a mere compliance with popular enthusiasm; but for educational enterprises, for churches building houses of worship, and especially to aid in their studies young men in whom were discerned the promise and potency of future usefulness in the ministry or otherwise, his tokens of sympathy were numerous, generous, and practical.

About the time he retired from business he built for himself a new and pleasant residence upon the site of the old one, two doors from the First Baptist Church. In this he resided the last fifteen years of his life, interesting himself in the education of his two young daughters, in the companionship of a large family circle, in the events transpiring in the religious world, and in a few business investments. Among the last was the enterprise of opening a new avenue through land which he had purchased. To this he gave his personal attention, completing it two years before his death.

In his family life he was firm, decided, but affectionate. He endeavored to impress upon his children the fear of God and devotion to his cause. Family worship was always observed by him, even to the last morning of his life. As a member of the church he was habitually present twice on the Lord's day and in the weekly prayer-meeting until his infirmities prevented. In the latter he often spoke or prayed, taking broad and hopeful views of the kingdom of Christ. He was a thoughtful and sympathizing helper of his pastors in Dayton. Not only the two deceased, whose names have already been mentioned, but Dr. S. W. Foljambe, now of Malden, Massachusetts, and Dr. H. Harvey, now of Madison Theological Seminary, and especially, the writer of this memoir found in him a valuable counselor. His long observation and ripe experience fitted him for this service. Having once been a minister himself, and conscious of his disposition to form and express decided opinions, he thought it the more delicate prudence not to participate much in the business meetings of the church. But he wished to be active in its spiritual work, and was always ready to testify concerning the grace of God.

He was not a voluminous correspondent. The habit of his mind was to seize upon practical rather than sentimental views of life. But no less pleasing to him on that account, in his advancing years, was an occasional exchange of letters with the friends of earlier days. Dr. Barnas Sears wrote to him from Staunton, Virginia: "It did me good to meet you at Buffalo and to talk over old times when we were young men, and such men as Grafton, Batchelder, Shepard, Bolles, and Sharp were the old men. In one thing we may both rejoice, the success of what was so near our hearts, ministerial education." Robert Ryland and Charles Thurber, the former a college mate at Columbian and the other at Brown, corresponded with him concerning their old classmates. Dr. Jonah G. Warren, from his retirement at Newton Center, poured out to him his heart in characteristic epistles, and Prof. S. S. Greene of Brown University wrote: "I should be most happy to do you any service that lies in my power. I do not forget the days long gone by when my course was guided not a little by your advice." To such letters his heart warmly responded. He greatly enjoyed a few years ago a visit from Dr. Ryland, and, more recently, visits from Dr. Basil Manly of the Southern Baptist Theological Seminary, who says: "My acquaintance with Dr. Thresher began more than forty years ago, when I went, in 1844, a youth of eighteen, to Newton Theological Institution. I found in his delightful family the most cordial reception, and the nearest substitute for the Alabama home I had left. His warm interest in the institution and in all who were connected with it, led him to be concerned for all students. But he seemed to show me special regard, probably because I was the youngest and farthest from home. The intimacy then established endured and strengthened through all the years, notwithstanding our remoteness in distance, and the infrequency of opportunities for meeting."

He wrote much for the religious press. He felt himself, he said, to be a relic of his own generation, and therefore could furnish out of his own early and extended acquaintance with religious leaders and organizations information and precedents of great value. His contributions to the *Journal and Messenger* would make a very large volume. A list of some of their topics will recall the nature of their contents; namely, *"Denison University, One Hundred Thousand Dollars Endowment,"* four articles; *"Talks About Our College,"* seven articles; *"Principles and Practices of Baptist Churches,"* fifteen articles; "*The American Bible Society and the Baptists*," two articles; "*The Relation of Bible Societies to Missions among the Heathen*," four articles; "*Bible Societies, their History*," four articles; "*Our Denominational Societies, What are They, and For What Purpose?*" six articles; "*The Great Bible Question Eliminated*," four articles; "*Paying for One's Education;*" "*Denominational Courtesy;*" "*Responsibility of Editors;*" "*The Church at Antioch;*" obituary articles on *Solomon Peck, J. T. Robert, Barnas Sears,* and *J. G. Binney; "One Hundred Years Ago;*" and a variety of contributions on benevolence, denominational principles, and methods of missionary organizations. Some of these, which were published in series, attracted considerable attention from thoughtful readers. His outspoken opinions could not please all, but the historical information and sober judgments which the articles contain make many of them permanently useful. Those who knew the age of the writer wondered at the evidence they gave of the prolonged vitality and acumen of his mental powers. Several occupying positions of great responsibility in the denomination kindly wrote to him expressing their gratitude for the service he had rendered with his pen.

On the twenty-fifth of June, 1884, he was again bereaved by the death of his wife. He was now nearly eighty-six years of age, and had great need of her thoughtful and tender care. She lived until their two daughters had completed their course in school, and, almost immediately after, was taken ill with the disease of which in a few days she died, greatly lamented by a large and loving circle of friends. Several times in his life he had been called to pass through deep affliction. Besides the cases already referred to in these pages, the deaths of Mrs. Mary L. Stilwell and Mrs. Sarah X. Crawford, who were his daughters, had brought great sorrow to his heart. In all these trials his faith in God had sustained him. That faith did not falter now, though the blow of this last affliction fell upon him when he was carrying the weight of years. The remarkable vigor of his faculties and the sympathizing attentions of the two daughters in his home, as well as of others, helped him to bear up under his grief. As cheerfully as possible, he maintained the spirit with which he first received the announcement to him of her departure: "I had confidently expected that she would see me through; but God has ordered otherwise, and I submit." He had always delighted to welcome public Christian workers to his house; and especially now did he enjoy the visit of his friend Rev. William Ashmore, D. D., for thirty-five years a missionary to China, whom he had invited to spend the winter under his roof.

With the exception of some deafness he retained to the end, to a remarkable degree, his physical and mental powers, reading in his library, walking to market, to the homes of his relatives and their places of business,

He made a journey to Granville about three months
before his death, and returned alone. He wished no one
to wait upon him. He would attend to his affairs himself, and no one could affirm that his mind was not clear
enough for the purpose. Only at intervals did it betray
any weakness. We shall not forget his venerable appearance, his snow-white hair and earnest look, as, swinging
his cane more as a precaution than as a support, he
moved briskly along the sidewalk. He expressed his
thoughts clearly and decidedly, and, unlike many aged
persons, talked not merely of the past but of things that
need to be done. The day before his death he was upon
the streets apparently in his usual vigor. On the morning of January 12, 1886, he sat at the breakfast table and
afterward in his library, cheerfully conversing with his
daughter. At the family worship that morning, with un-
realized appropriateness, the seventh chapter of the Reve-
lation had been read, closing with the words: "Therefore
are they before the throne of God, and serve him day and
night in his temple: and he that sitteth on the throne
shall dwell among them. They shall hunger no more,
neither thirst any more; neither shall the sun light on
them, nor any heat. For the Lamb which is in the
midst of the throne shall feed them, and shall lead
them unto living fountains of waters: and God shall
wipe away all tears from their eyes." His own voice
had led them as usual in simple petitions at the Throne
of Grace. He had spoken of walking out, but had been

11

dissuaded by his daughter on account of the severity of the weather. Before noon he expected to ride to a meeting of some gentlemen on business in which he was interested. No premonition of approaching death was observable till he suddenly complained of feeling ill and almost immediately became unconscious. Lying upon a lounge in the library where he had so often entertained his visitors, he lingered for an hour or two, during which his loved ones gathered sorrowfully around him, and then he gently breathed his last. The messenger he had long been expecting had come suddenly. Paralysis had stopped the functions of life when his mind was clear and his heart was peaceful. Thus his family were spared the distress of witnessing a lingering illness. Comparatively without physical pain he left them, and went "to be with Christ, which is far better."

He lived a long life—eighty-seven years, four months, and twelve days. He was born before the death of George Washington. He lived under the administration of every other president of the United States. He was spared to see the population of the land multiplied tenfold. In his childhood there were no railroads, no cheap postal-system, no ocean steamships, no electric telegraphs, no Sunday-schools, no religious newspapers, and none of the vast improvements, material or moral, which these have brought in their train. He survived to watch the passing by of an immense procession of his fellow-men. Scarcely ever before in the history of

the world have eighty-seven years included so many
and such sublime events as he was permitted to wit-
ness.

And now little need be added to that view of his
character which the mere story of his life presents.
We have seen that he was a man of independent judgment and persistent will. Slow in forming his opinions,
he yet formed them thoughtfully and strongly, and then
adhered to them to the end. Nor did he hesitate to
declare them in the most outspoken manner. In this
he may sometimes have seemed partial and severe. The
very qualities which made him so strong may at times
have made him exacting and autocratic. Some may have
thought him overconservative. But he was remarkably broad-minded and progressive in all his thoughts
and plans for the interests of truth and righteousness.
He believed in laying foundations deep and building
for the future. He thus kept his heart young, and was
an encouragement to others to go on and do more.
While the directness and strong feeling with which he
pursued his chosen aims were not always pleasing to
others, and may at times have prejudiced his mind, conversation with him always disclosed a desire to be just,
and his life as a whole was marked with great courtesy
and kindness.

His faith in Christ was humble and tender. In 1882
he wrote to Dr. Ryland: "In recent years Christ has
been increasingly exalted in my thoughts and affections

as I have contemplated his marvelous work of redemption, and my relation to him as a sinner saved. It has seemed to me that all that he did and suffered was necessary for my salvation. Yet so marvelous is his grace, that 'he is able also to save them to the uttermost that come unto God by him, seeing he ever liveth to make intercession for them.' I feel a constant need of his forgiving mercy. This also has been to me a comforting promise: 'Because I live, ye shall live also.'" Such Christian convictions and hopes had much to do in shaping Dr. Thresher's whole course. The doctrines of grace furnished motives to his conduct. "Delighting in the law of the Lord," he was "like a tree planted by the rivers of water." This world would be a happy place if as much loyalty to Christ could be found in all lives as he was wont to manifest. A large number can adopt as an expression of their own feelings regarding him the language of President Alvah Hovey, who writes: "My own acquaintance with him has been a source of unalloyed pleasure to me. His sound judgment, his consistent piety, his warm interest in missions, his just appreciation of Christian education, his broad and enlightened views on all the great questions that concern the kingdom of God and the welfare of mankind, made his conversation delightful and profitable; and his brave and hopeful spirit was at all times inspiring."

The funeral took place on the afternoon of Thursday,

January 14, 1886. Dr. William Ashmore offered a prayer at the house. Then the casket was borne to the church close by, where a large audience had assembled of the relatives, business associates, church-members, and friends of the deceased, and where it was placed before the pulpit between ripe sheaves and with a crown of flowers upon it. Dr. Basil Manly of the Southern Baptist Theological Seminary, and President Alfred Owen of Denison University participated in the services. The pastor of the deceased paid a loving tribute to his memory, appropriate hymns were sung, and afterward the remains were borne to their resting-place in Woodland Cemetery.

To two sons and three daughters surviving him he has left the precious legacy of his Christian counsel and example. "*Being dead, he yet speaketh.*" Through these pages may his life speak, as well as in the memories of those who knew him! It is a profitable thing to trace the path of such a man. In our endeavor to do so we have glanced also at many other "foot-prints on the sands of time"—foot-prints which, like his, direct us to the "city that hath foundations, whose builder and maker is God."